I0457600

The Last Dragon's egg

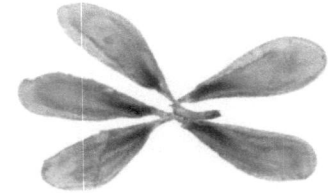

Brian Dry

Copyright © Brian Dry 2019. All rights reserved. No part of this publication may be reproduced, stored in a retrieval system, or transmitted in any form or by any means without the prior written permission of the publisher, nor be circulated in any form of binding or cover other than that which it is published and without a similar condition being imposed on the subsequent purchaser

Publisher: Brian Dry ISBN: 978-0-6481282-7-4

Cover and internal art by Brian Dry.

Table of contents

Contents

Characters and Worlds

Tandiette: Daughter of Ashland, A princess to a throne if legends are real

Parian: Brother to Tandiette.

Claritine: Stepmother to Tandiette.

Dominico: Tandiette's home country on Virgon.

Virgon: Home world surrounded by two moons that share the same atmosphere.

Tidan moon: Ashland's home world.

Grey moon: Once known for its beautiful rich culture and forrests. Also known in times of old, as Poorus.

Ductile: Flying creature. Not to be messed with if one values their fingers.

Unworthy: One infectious ugly critter.

Biscuit: one hot baked cookie with an unusual taste.

Radian: A little mischief.

Destructor: What a Kreton, keep out of the way, least you be flattened.

Dearling: love dark places.

Halfling: Half Dearling, half something else... but one could be wrong?

Seraphina: A captured soul with a past she wants to hide.

Devlin: Bad to the bone.

The Grand Rous: King of the Dearlings.

Arogon: Bird of a different feather.

Sir Erin: Trust no one.

The Light Barrier: A curtain of thick bright swirling goup, one must never breathe in if they know what's good for them.

Raval: Lost to a delirium that tasted so good.
Penrite: A stone fired in a volcano's hell, so tough diamond took second place.
Sunny Bill: A name only used by Ashland when he is extremely displeased with someone. ∞∞∞∞

Chapter 1

Home

Pushed the princess ran, long hair matted, face muddied. She was the end of the line for her gene pool and in her hands, she carried the last dragon's egg. Dominicon her country and without her the surrounding hordes would demolish it, like every other country on this world.

A clang, her face turned, she knew the noise well as the branches scratched her legs, but above all she held the prize, warm, close to her heart. It too had a heart, synchronized with her beat, an attachment so strong even the clang of the hording beasts couldn't dim and she felt the crack. Broken, the shell, not from the beasts, but from her love and she heard a baby's first growl. Joined now with her symbiont her eyes glowed red and she withdrew her breath of fire.

Two moons looked down. The blue glow unchanged in ten centuries. Ten centuries without a queen and if the prophet's dire predictions true, not for another ten. She stepped into its glow and felt the blue rays cool the fire in her body. The hordes surrounded her, their din of shields against armour. They would have to wait for her symbiont was too young for battle yet.

'Tandiette over here,' she swivelled to a shrubs lift, her body sliding the last three feet, dirt with branches followed and down she fell into the tunnel. Up above the bush was ripped from the ground and she and Parian were running like they had never run before. The rattle of armour mere metres behind, closing. Parian ripped at a loose root and with a mighty thump the earth behind collapsed along with a horde of whatever would fit. 'Fate,' he said, 'the sweet sound of fate,' and he coughed out the thick black dust as he looked to her. Likehart glowed, dripping with beads of golden orbs in her presence.

She smiled, 'You fool that was our only way out.'
'No Tandiette we have been busy,' and he pressed on the rock ahead to see the boulder roll like a marble and her radiance, the light, as they entered.
The smell of ten thousand lichen flooded their nostrils, full with the musty taste of moss and earthly aftertones, which meant, the separation from the ground dwellers was permanent. Tandiette gazed ahead to a maze of caverns lit by a million tiny glow domes.
'This way Tandiette,' and she followed, her baby's claws digging in as it clung, humming soft groans in unison to the glow domes illumination, only to dull once more as they passed. Ahead, a new home, other Dearlings approaching with news of her return spreading.
'Out of my way,' her stepmother pushing through, the twins Roselyn and Riesel close behind. So, what have you done with your father?' eyes straining in the lack of light.
'I left him on Tidan. He insisted.'
'Insisted did he,' and she pushed at the Dearling closest as if it was his fault. Claritine her stepmother didn't share the draculetic pointy teeth, nor the large eyes of too long below and she was always smugly frightful to the

squeak of a bat in the dark. She was a full Tidan unlike her siblings. They were Halflings to a different father, or so she was told, but they shared little of a Tidan's traits.

'Yes, where is Ashland?' her stepsisters said as one.

Tandiette ignored the request, irritated by their need to use his Tidan name when he had a perfectly good Dominicon one. On another world her father could be a saint, but here an alien, with all the weirdness, an apple amongst the lemons, her memories not so distant. She knew all too well how different she felt when she was just a Youngling. How the other Dearlings would tease her. For the pain of being different deeply embedded, not one thing or another. A low growl escaped from beneath her coat.

'What have we here,' Claritine said.

Parian looked at Tandiette who shook her pointy ears like they had a touch of cottonmoss. 'Um it is only my stomach.' She said, 'I haven't eaten in days. Could you please show me where we have moved the food to Parian,' as a noise erupted from another part of her body.

'Oh you Halflings are such disgusting creatures,' Claritine said. Roselyn and Reisel's pointy ears drooped. 'Not you two,' she added. 'You look like a true Dominicon, not like poor Tandiette here, and she smiled satisfied.

'This way,' Parian said and she followed. 'So you have it then, the egg?'

Tandiette looked around. 'Not here, remember what father told us.'

'I know a place,' and they passed through the giant marble cathedral, stalagmites holding like two gods of a lost past. The tunnel smelt of rotten eggs, a place no one wanted to linger, safe from prying noses.

Opening out they looked down to the belly of the beast. Red fire rocks melted to splatters of bubbling molten rock, invading the air with a breath so hot they both stepped back as they watched the cinders rise a full mile to the mouth of the volcano, only to cool with the blue of Tidan above.

Tandiette checked they were alone before, 'No egg anymore, look.'

'By wizard, by light of the moons, it can't be real?'

'Real as a bats bite,' and she stroked her creature like a new mother would.

A beam of blue moon drifted across the entrance above, moving slowly, illuminating all but a foot of ground where they stood, but it was enough.

'Awool,' her tiny creature howled, engrained with a need so determined only one person on three worlds could cure.

'Shh,' Tandiette said and its big green eyes looked deep into hers, searching for a need. 'Shh my darling, I feel it too, we will find you food.'

'Food, what kind of food can it eat?'

She knew but they were a little too big to fit in her baby's mouth just yet. They set forth, the winding passages greeted with glow domes and wild mushrooms. Up ahead she stopped and picked a handful and began to feed her dragon.

'Yuk,' Parian said. 'How can it eat that stuff raw?'

'It is like feeding a carnivore, a substitute for what he really craves.'

'Like a Vege-burger... Hey you said "he," how do you know it's a he? Here let me check,' and with one snap Parian's fingers were pulled away close to disappearing with what a dragon really craves. 'God that thing is

4

dangerous,' checking he still had all three fingers and thumb.

Tandiette opened her hand and let her dragon devour the mushroom with a knowing that a dragon would never bite the hand that feeds him.

'So then, when do we, see father again,' Parian said.

She turned from wiping her baby's mouth and looked deep into her brother's eyes. 'He loves you as much as me Parian.'

'I know, but when?'

'He is in a difficult position on Tidan, made worse by what is happening here on Virgon.'

'When?' Parian insistent.

'Four weeks, when Tidan is directly overhead again. The commanders up there are hard to fool. He has to be careful, least we be found out.

They walked on, deep in a knowing, to keep this secret they would have to venture into the wastelands, where no Dearling would go. Parian's scars moved with his body, reaching out of his shirt and down the back of his arm like a crayon monster had drawn lines to a point of no return. He coughed and spat the taste in his mouth, noxious fumes invading every sinus. Tight volcanic rocks reached out to touch their skin.

'Damn stupid of father to think we would be able to keep a baby dragon safe.'

'Parian, we have to try for father,' she paused '… and mother.'

'Your mother, not mine.'

She hesitated and wiped the tear.

'You brought her up not me,' Parian said. 'Come on.'

'How do we know? Is it safe?'

'We don't.'

5

Ahead the passage ceased. A veil of pure energy glistened, he rubbed his scar for luck and pushed through the curtain of light. Twelve feet and they held their breaths, because to breathe the light meant a little piece might linger. She put the thought out of her head, her hand firmly clasped over her baby's mouth and nose as they emerged. A million lights filled her head like stars in the night, her eyes adjusting to see as well as her brother, for she was not one thing or another. Up above, as they broke from the barrier, the beginnings of an ocean spread out. The light they passed through, nature's barrier, to hold the waters up and not swallow them whole.

'Why do they call this place the wastelands?' Parian said.

'Father said it was because of a time, very long past, when dragons roamed like bats in the night.' They looked out to the dense vegetation, thick with jungle vines and tall plants. Far off a creature's call soaked through.

'Very big bats I would guess?'

Tandiette patted her little dragon who had already outgrown the egg. They followed the path worn long ago, vegetation encroaching on every turn.

'This is where father taught Ismelda, wasn't it?' Parian said, wiping droppings from his sandal. 'Ductiles like her need all the respect they can get what with that large head full of teeth. I don't know how you and father can fly her?'

'Dreams Parian, so vivid they would make our pointy ears tune to the impossible.'

'Not fathers, he looks as Tidan as Claritine.'

Tandiette stared ahead, ignoring the comment. 'We have to make plans, a safe place, somehow keep our regular lives together, without... Oh it all seems impossible.' She heard the soothing growl from beneath

6

her coat once more and looked deep into her baby's emerald green eyes. 'Don't worry we will find a way.' Her dragon's pupils turned to slits, searching between the gap in her shirt as a brother's ears twitched annoyed, like all the times in the past when he was ignored, or was there something else?

The single path snaked past the dense vegetation and what was once far off, broke close. The cry unmistakable as Parians ears froze, his scar rising on the back of his arm from a memory. 'Ductile, Ductile,' he yelled and they ran, but too late… the dribbling mouth opened to show the saliva drip from the beasts dagger-teeth, powerful legs crouched blocking the path, which only meant one thing; attack.

Frozen unable to utter a single word they stood eye to eye as the creature's tongue tasted their last breath and when every muscle in its body was about to pounce, a shrill cry broke the air, so shattering, all who heard stood, paralysed. The Ductile halted on the track and stared. Its squinting glare eased as the saliva dried to their relief and twelve feet of its wings opened, flying feathers in a single flap rising before looking down to unfriendly eyes, only to lift again on the subterranean breeze that flowed from a world apart and the heat of glare emanating from an infant and his adopted mother. An infant breathed easy, no need for a second warning, he thought.

'Well I'll be a Ductiles dinner, if that don't beat all,' Parian said.

'You're a special little thing, aren't you my little… We'll have to give you a name, won't we, but first things first. Now what did father say about directions? Ideas Parian?'

'How should I know? That thing we just saw had me running for my life on my previous attempt and I have the scars to prove it.'∞∞∞∞

Chapter 2

'Remember to keep the beany pulled down over your ears Tandiette.'

'Yes father.' She felt for the hand knitted cap with all four fingers, her thumb catching on the inside with an embroidered name.

'You look as beautiful as your mother,' he said.

'Dad!' her look was enough and they both knew the reason. Any other course of action meant discovery, with her mother lost like so many before her, and she told herself; it was not too late.

The city rose up from the blue glow that gave Tidan her name. The swamp impenetrable if not for the cobblestone roads that led in, or a creature that could fly like a bat, not to mention bite one's head off, if it had a mind to. They had Ismelda tied to a rock three miles back, nibbling on some toads, her favourite.

Two guards stood beyond the lowered drawbridge, rough underfoot, through the wooden cracks, open mouths of water-serpents stopped momentarily to see if it was feeding time.

'Now remember, from here on you're my servant Tandiette, nothing more.'

'How many times, I'm not a child anymore.' He smiled and gave her the pack to carry. The guards ahead unaware, busy laughing at the scraps they threw on the ripples of the moat below, only to disappear in a splash.

'Morning gentlemen,' Ashland said.

Startled they looked up... 'Captain Crosswell,' their swords once swinging by their side, stilled and in unison they saluted.

'At ease,' Ashland said as they walked on and into the busy market. Stalls of fruit on the left, to the right hides of animals hung drying while a maker busied himself with the leather. A young boy ran past with a gousnip, the fruit so ripe the very drips tasted of sweet reward.

'Stop thief,' a merchant roared.

A guard looked down from the thick wall, 'Louie, Hippo, stop that kid!'

Silence befell the once noisy market. Burley big bodies stood with hands of iron ready to grab, but as they grasped, a child ducked and weaved, fruit spilling in every direction. One guard pulled his sword as the nimble feet of a thief bested the weapon ringing to hands that struck nothing but petrified ancient wood. 'No you don't, you little devil,' he shouted.

'You couldn't hit a bush pig in a barnyard, Hippo. Here let me,' and the other guard reached for the well coiled rope hanging loose at his side. Two hard dried nuts the size of under ripe melons whistled on each end, above his head, as he let fly. Twenty feet, almost to the end of the drawbridge, it found the little thief. Feet wrapped like a chicken ready to be plucked. Desperate lemons rocked to the lament of what could have been, only to rest between the cracks of outstretched fingers and a child's cry of what will come.

Hippo grasped the lariat and lifted the child, dangling him over the moat. 'Feeding time my dearies,' he rasped. The child thief's eyes said what he couldn't before, then…

'It's not my fault mister. My baby brother and sister are starving… please… All I'm doing is trying to feed the family.'

Hippo's grip tightened… 'Maybe the quartz mine,' and he cast the little one to sprawl to a crumpled mess at his feet.

Tandiette turned to her father, 'We have to do something,' quietly pulling on his sleeve. Tugging, he gave her the, "I can't interfere"stare" she'd seen so many times before, but this time something was different. 'Father please,' and at once he turned, for she had broken the never to be broken rule. He checked to see if anyone

11

had heard, while before him his daughter's determined stare remained unchanged.

'Hold up men,' Ashland yelled and from the midst of the crowd they emerged.

Tandiette beside her father as she looked at a brute's feet, then to the boy. Her tear salted by a cry from a distant memory, when a mother's body lay twisted, piled with arms and legs exposed to raw words. 'This is what happens when we find a liar,' she heard, burned by the recollection of her mother's love being broken.

'But, Captain Crosswell,'cried Louie confused, as he looked over to Hippo, whose face was the colour of a wild red radish. 'This little "Crit" had us all scrambling, not to mention the market owner's loss, and everyone knows this example must be dealt with.'

'Then I shall deal with it, soldier.'

'But?'

'No,' and Ashland turned his focus from the two and looked down to the boy. 'If I untie this thing, you must promise, not to run… Otherwise, I will not help when the river serpents are munching on your bones. Is that understood?' The boy shook his head with the guard's faces bursting to beyond restraint until they saw their Captains frown. 'There is a debt to be paid just the same,' and he led the child back into the marketplace. 'Who here has the child stolen from?' he demanded.

A rumble of voices echoed in the crowd… 'Me Sir,' the stall owner said as he hobbled toward them, withered by time in the fields.

'Take me to your stall,' Ashland said as he looked around to the empty stocks, a rare thing he thought.

'What are you going to do…fa… master?' Tandiette whispered.

He ignored his daughter and said, 'So this produce is all yours?'

'Yes Sir.'

He squeesed the juice out of a tomatoe.'I shall purchase this basket of tomatoes and you boy.' Ashland looked down to the child thief, 'You boy will be locked in those stocks... yonder... and every day for a week the storeowner will throw two tomatoes from his stall at you, no more, no less, until this basket is empty.'

'But sir I'm not that accurate. I might, god forbid, hit some poor soul walking past.'

'Then you should learn to protect your property more securely, shouldn't you,' Ashland said.

A bell rang, not loud, but just loud enough. From beneath a stone building his rough exterior appeared. One eye closed by a wound that crept from eyebrow to lip. 'Who rings the jailor's bell,' he said.

Everyone stepped back... 'Me!' Ashland said. 'This lad has a week in the stocks. No more, no less, and the only person to apply a punishment is this stall owner.'

'Come lad,' and the jailor led the boy away as the marketplace returned to normal.

'Is he a bad boy,' a little girl asking her mother?

'Yes,' she replied.

Ashland turned to his daughter before she had time to contemplate the little thief's fate and pointed... Ahead the grand hall of the castle... Cold marble echoed on every step, empty this time of day. They climbed the curling staircase to the second floor. At the end, a room waited, theirs. The heavy wood creaked to his strong hand as Ashland twisted the old lock and they were free from prying ears.

'How can we even locate mother?'

'Tandiette we are not alone in this, there is still time. How goes the training of the little one?'

'Do you know where mother is?'

'Anything I say is for our protection. Today for example if anyone overheard you calling me father. You know what's at stake…'

'But the boy, I couldn't just stand back.'

'So much of your mother in you,' he paused. 'That boy is more important than he realises and you Tandiette are not to have any contact with him. Is that understood? Here I have a book for you to read.'

'A book? You know how I feel about reading. She looked down to the title, "The Extinction of Palientoscites, or Common Dragon."

'Oh,' she said.

'I have to go out. The word is, The Council of Five are meeting here tonight and I need to be prepared. I will send a servant with food. All you have to do is stay put and I will see you later, and we can discuss the little-ones training.'

The door closed. Time was cold and meaningless away from home. Virgon shone so large through the open window she could almost reach out and touch it, but inside, the stones of the castle needed an open fire to warm. She opened the book. A fully grown dragon, majestic in full flight, covered both pages. Flicking on she read the words, violent, fire breathing devils and as she turned to the last page, she saw a once beautiful creature, slain. The word extinct covering the body with no apology. Flames flickered on the walls growing with evil intent before they exploded with the cinders of failure. She stoked the fire again. I will not be beaten, she told herself as a commotion outside her window drew her interest. She looked down.

'Take that,' a boy throwing mud at the child thief whose arms were useless, trapped by the stocks of heavy timber. His face the colour of mud.

'Stop!' Tandiette yelled unable to contain what she really was.

'Who says?' The bully looked up. 'A servant girl has no say, do they,' and to prove a point he gathered another handful of mud and threw. Thick the mud caused the little thief to splutter for breath.

'Bully!' Tandiette yelled, persecution a piece of her, rebelling deep, like the red of her hair. Her eyes alight where every rule a father said was but mud on the bottom of her sandal. She could almost hear the wishes of ghosts as she ran down the staircase with the echo of her soles all that remained. Outside the stallholders packing up, some left already. The bully laughing with a small group of his friends unaware of her approach, until, one pointed her out.

She walked past them and dipped a scarf in the water trough. 'We are not all without compassion,' she whispered to the child thief, wiping his face clean. The hand she felt reach for her beany was meant as a taunt, but for every reason in her world she reacted. The silver fleck on her skin shone to the scales of an ancient justice and she punched the hand away, her secret almost intact. She checked her beany as she looked the bully full in the face.

'Servant girl, you have no say here. Get back to your cleaning or whatever meaningless task fills your pitiful little life,' he said.

Her tongue swam like a serpent in her mouth wanting to whip the meanness from his words, but she just clenched her jaw, because there was another way, and she turned and walked away. The smirk on his face applauded by his friends, that was, until they heard the bell... Tandiette rang it again, louder this time.

'Who rings the jailor's bell,' his good eye casting a glare on the petite girl standing by the annoyance.

'I do,' she spat almost dribbling to an indigestible taste, or was it a need.

'Go on.'

'These... These...' She didn't know what they were, caught in a cross between fully grown men and underfed children. 'These idiots... have just thrown mud all over your responsibility and are laughing at your rules,' she said. Three bullies stepped back, to blend with whatever people were left in the marketplace, silenced by her words.

Telling the jailor his responsibilities was one step too far, not because he was twice her size or she could smell him from twenty feet, but his reputation meant he had the tough, raw grime to go with it. 'So, servant girl, point out who throws mud over my rules?'

Tandiette looked around, but for the life of her she couldn't see one of them. It was as if they had vanished. 'I'm sorry sir but they've disappeared. They must have run off.'

'Run off have they. Then who shall pay for this annoyance,' and without another word he approached. Every scense overpowered as two large hands wrapped her arms. Shocked she was about to fight back, to the glares of storeholders. They would see what she was and she knew all her father's careful plans were in ruin, along with any chance of rescue for her mother. 'Maybe a night in the stocks along with your little friend will help,' and with her body at his whim, his practised touch slammed

16

the wooden cage closed over her neck as she thought she heard the snicker of a bully.

He moved to the front of the stocks about to remove her beany to show who disrespected his authority. His large thumb grasped an edge of her beany and he saw. She thought his big black eye winked or was he just playing a cruel game, but he stopped and pulled her beany down again turning to the stallholders and in a voice that ripped to the edges of his gravel tone he said. 'Anyone who approaches or even touches these two, will feel the taste of my rack.' He scanned the half dozen remaining stallholders with his good eye. 'Anyone.' Was that a smile on his lips as he stared again into her face, or was she simply dreaming?

∞∞∞∞

The castle's grand library held a secret, deep in its bowels. A door. He felt for his watch, a habit from a forgotten past, cherished in the skills passed down by his father, a master craftsman of mechanics. He pressed on the secret panel and waited for the mechanics to do their job as the hidden room revealed itself. At the centre, a table stood with chairs for the Council of Five, four occupied.

'Sorry for the delay,' he said as he seated himself at the head of the table. 'A little problem needed my attention.' Grumbles of the four, fresh, as he waited patiently knowing they would settle. His crown so distant, strangled by decades of mindboggling events, but once, tied to something ancient and forgotten. In the other chairs, Erin, George, William and Lauren. Titles lost with their lands.

'They are reinforcing the numbers on Virgon as we speak,' Ashland began.

17

'The grey moons riches exhausted, polluted, the atmosphere now toxic for them to breath, I suspect,' Erin said.

'Oh, poppycock Sir Erin. I believe the silk cloth of a fine handkerchief would be enough to unclog a lung,' Lauren replied.

'We are powerless. He has divided us and stripped away the loyalties we once held. Sometimes I feel helpless and wonder if all is lost,' William said.

'Poppycock, poppycock and more poppycock, as long as we five breathe a breath, there is always hope. How goes your search for Seraphina, Ashland?' Lauren said.

'Funny you should ask. A lad, now residing in our stocks, awaits. His village targeted by a renegade element of our devils reign. To date I don't know why, but I am looking into the matter personally, which reminds me I am late, very late and apologise because I must go.' Ashland lifted the lid on his family heirloom, never on time, but little of his life was.

Tandiette looked up from her stock. The heavy wood biting into her wrists. A cast iron lock bolted closed with the key hanging securely around their jailors neck. The bright of night lit by the grey moon's presence. If she strained she could almost see the campfires of the work camps. Her mother captive out there, so close and yet so far.

'So servant girl what makes you stick up for me?' the child thief said.

'I would do the same for anyone in your position.'

'Maybe,' looking down as his neck raw from the wooden restraint, 'but I know no one will come for me, my family taken by force to the grey moon's mines.'

18

'What, you said they were starving, that's why you stole.'

'How could you know what it takes to survive? I look to the dark sky knowing no one can fix the plight of my brother and sister on the shine of a soulless moon.'

'My mother also,' Tandiette stopped, silent for a moment, wrestling to a place of comfort. 'When I was a child the hours my brother and I sat with mother looking up. So much beauty here, on the blue of Tidan, so much future. The stories she would tell of princes with realms, of tyrants and champions held by pride and privilege and wealth. Tonight, all I see is torment and hell, any wealth of knowledge is only but a bell for the privilege to sell.'

'Fancy words for a servant girl, but I don't understand. You said looking up to the blue. Don't you mean the grey of Poorus because we are on the blue of Tidan,' and as he said the words his lips smiled at the dirt below. 'There are stories in my village, words spoken around a campfire of a legend. One who will take on the might of our enemy. Born one of our three worlds, who speaks the ancient's language to beasts and Tidans alike, able to bend the well of knowledge at will. We wait his arrival,' and Tandiette thought she saw him smirk.

'Her arrival,' she replied.

'Tandiette, what on blazes?' A voice echoing through her pointy ears. 'Don't tell me how, we will discuss this later.' Ashland eyed the cast iron lock and said, 'Don't move a muscle. I shall return,' and he walked off.

'Masters not happy,'she heard.

'Oh shut up, this is all your fault.'

'Me?'

She stared at the ground not knowing what would happen and without another word from anyone, her lock fell open, by the jailors hand himself, and trouble was her companion once again. ∞∞∞∞

Chapter 3

A name

Parian snapped his hand away before fingers were sandwiched between loving jaws, or so he tried to remind himself.

'No Biscuit, I haven't anymore,' he said. Biscuit eyed him, two smoke rings drifted ominous from flared nostrils as he clawed at the rock wall before rolling his back against the indents, scratching at the annoyance of scales. Flakes fell like shredded rocky shale, to line the cave floor.

'I have to go.'

Biscuit groaned, unnerving Parian, only one of his latest changes. When size matters Biscuit was still a minnow in this place, but for some other reason the wildlife didn't seem to bother with Parians constant comings and goings. So, he returned like every other time, barely missed by the Dearlings or Claritine.

High above a volcano, circling, Ashland pulled the reigns on Ismelda and they dropped like cold stones to the heart of the beast. 'Wait, wait,' he yelled into Ismelda's ear, red ash whistling past to stinging eyes, feathers and bodies alike. 'Whoa,' he yelled to a sharp pull on the reigns and Ismelda opened her wings to the full ferocity of the volcano for a split second, and with a second tug they landed out of reach. Tandiette's stroke soothed the smouldering wing feathers, eyes one with Ismelda's, cooling her thoughts.

'She'll be fine. Two weeks is time enough for her to mend,' Ashland said.

'Surely there's another way?'

'We dare not risk with what roams above,' and as they turned, in the entrance, Parian.

'Welcome home,' he said. 'I bet you can't wait to find out?'

'Not here,' the taste of rotten eggs in their mouths as they walked on, a thousand yards and out into moist air. Rock walls rising, trapped by the stalactite filled ceiling two hundred feet up… Dearlings busy, carrying lumps of petrified wood as they crossed the expanse. On the far side, in a doorway, Claritine waited.

'Took your time. Why am I the last to know of your return; Darling?' Tandiette's nose twitched like she wanted to scratch something, but resisted, and walked past her stepmother to see what their new home was like.

'I have something for you Claritine,' as Tandiette's head spun. Ashland carefully removed the dark stone from his pocket, gold claws clinging to the gem. Dangled, threaded in a fine chain, Claritine's stare overcome by his kiss to a cheek as he carefully placed it over her head. She smiled at Tandiette, whose thoughts were as pure as a lizard trapped by the cat.

'So, what's to eat?' Parian said.

'Nothing, big boys get their own breakfast, don't they, twins?' The twin's smile almost reaching their pointy ears as Ashland scooped them up. One under each arm and they giggled like they were toddlers again. 'My how you've grown,' and he threw them swirling into the air, 'two foot two, tadpoles no more.' Reaching, he squirmed "Phew…"

'Twins stop annoying your father… So, Darling,' and she looked at Tandiette again, 'this isn't one of those dark rubies from that depraved moon, is it?' Claritine studying her gift more closely.

'Do you mind if it is?'

'Of course not, but, twins can you two run off and wash, no scrub, the whole thing carefully with disinfectant. She lifted the jewel over her head and gave it to them. 'One never knows what I'm likely to catch, does one; isn't that right Tandiette?'

Tandiette screwed her nose and bit her bottom lip, a common trait of late, and said. 'I'll let Parian show me around, isn't that right little brother?'

'As long as it involves food,' and they walked off with the point of their ears straight up. 'They've just opened, "a new eats," and I'm dying to try some of the grub.'

Three Dearlings were stringing up a sign spelt out in the wild black of their language, Crow's Feet. Lines were long, crowded inside, but Tandiette didn't care, she was hungry, patience burned in seconds as she looked to see what part of an animal set her juices turning. A group of vegetarians sat at the table next to them, she admired their purpose, but she was made from different origins with needs she had little control over.

'So what do you think of the bats wing burger?'

Tandiette chewed another bite and looked at the vegetarians seated next to her. 'I don't know, I think we need more vegans', and she frowned because she wasn't sure if what she meant was more vegetable or Dearling.

Parian laughed bemused, 'You know what walks above calls us a delicacy.'

Confused, she hoped her feelings didn't show, or worse, were a sign. 'So how goes my little one?'

Parian looked around, 'I've given him a name.'

'A name?'

'Yes,' his fingers and thumb entwined with his other hand like they were protected, 'Biscuit.'

'What type of name is that, all you think of is your stomach. Come let's go and meet... Biscuit.'

'Shouldn't we wait for father?'

'He knows where we'll be and I'm sure Claritine has plans for him.'

Off they set through the tangle of winding tunnels, a home for the time being.

'This path is becoming so overgrown,' Tandiette said. Up ahead they heard growls, the likes of which she had never heard before. 'What's that,' her hand halting Parian in his tracks.

'That's your baby dragon, sounds like he's pleased to smell you.'

They rounded the last vine. He stood waiting, all six feet, smoke drifting from each nostril.

'Gosh he's grown, and so fast.' Hesitant she held out her hand. A forked tongue the size of her arm slid out and licked her fingers. She smiled, every sense in her body alive with his love, and as she stroked, growls of affection turned to coughs of dark smoke. He coughed the black stuff out again.

'He must have a cold, or it could be his way of growing, unlike you Tandiette, too old to be called a Youngling any longer,' Parian said.

'Have you been looking after him right,' Tandiette's eyes turning annoyed.

'That's right blame me, leaving all the shit jobs, no offense Biscuit,' Parian keeping his hands firmly to himself, 'while you and father go gallivanting off, living it up on Tidan.'

'You have no idea what Tidan is like, and I'm not going to explain what we do,' she stopped, looking at Biscuit with smoke drifting from his direction. 'He seems healthy enough other than this smoke business. I wonder what that's about.'

'I hear the apology, but I don't hear the... Thankyou Parian for risking your life to take care of my dragon... do I?'

'Thankyou little brother,' she said, eye to eye like all rival siblings.

Biscuit groaned again and started his daily ritual of rubbing his back against the rock wall. She went over and stroked her dragon's face, a full foot taller than her. Biscuit reached out with his front paw, claws gently resting on her. She ran her hand down his body to the annoyance of where the scales met the eruption of nodules.

'Parian what do you think these ridges are?'

'Stuffed if I know, you're the one, supposedly, with all the knowledge.'

Her mind was empty, except she remembered back to the book her father had given, if she'd only taken an interest. 'There was a book, never mind, a picture... that showed dragons with wings... I wonder?' Biscuit groaned again as he rubbed the annoyance, and coughed. Black smoke swallowed Parian. She saw two pointy ears and she thought she saw reddened eyes as he ran for a breath of moist air.

Then between the smoky haze. 'Sorry I'm late. How is our little dragon faring?' Ashland's silhouette illuminated in the entrance.

'Father I knew you'd come,' Tandiette said. Biscuit growled deep. A warning. 'Stop it you naughty thing.'

Parian nudged their father,' I'd keep your hands well away from the mouth. I do,' Parian said.

'So, let me, take a look, at him,' and out from the back of the cave, led by Tandiette, her dragon walked upright and clumsy. 'Gosh he's nearly as tall as me,' Ashland said, and before he could say another word her dragon breathed in.

'He's going to cough,' Parian cried as he ran for the entrance, but Biscuit just breathed out and leant forward, his nostrils flaring filling his lungs with every scent of Ashland; and before anyone could say anything he extended his front paw to the ground and bowed like he knew the meaning to a long lost reason.∞∞∞∞

Chapter 4

Mother

She looked at another broken nail and bit down on the end. Dirt tasted of nothing, she was one with the mess. Melinda on the other trestle bed, asleep, clothes shredded, mere threads of an exquisite disease. The whole place reeked of it and if frustration was ever present, this germ had buried her resistance long ago. Greed needs a master and she was submerged within the whole mess. What beauty, eroded, leaching to the edges of her beloved moon until the soul bled black. Slop, they called food, pushed away, under her bunk for later when she could stomach.

The camps were guarded by The Unworthy. She peered through the flap in the tent, two buildings partially obscured as an oversized hand sent shivers pointing to clawed fingernails playing a card game. Grotesque voices of retched laughter reaching, she dabbed the root lotion on the latest scab, and wondered, what Melinda had done to acquire such a treasure. Melinda stirred with the sound. Blotched pure white skin wrinkled to sooted thread red eyes. 'Please don't ask,' Melinda whispered with Seraphina's hand recapping the bottle.

'Never mind. All we have to do is stay alive for another day Melinda,' but words were but tears in a desert and she felt the end was coming fast, they all did, the slaves that was. She looked out again. The dust of the diggers settled for the night and her precious memories of a green home world all but gone. She pulled the muck from beneath the bed and forced herself to take a mouthful, 'You should do the same Melinda.'

'I don't think I can.'

'We need to keep what strength we can, there is always hope… hope with what we have found.'

'How can an egg help us, even if they have smuggled it out, especially without a word since.'

'Silence can be a sign. I don't know how I know, but I have this feeling, somewhere out there a baby is stirring.'

From beneath another part of her bed she pulled a pot. Inside five shoots of green. She pushed aside the dirt and poured the remainder of her daily water ration.

'You must be crazy to waste what is so precious on those seeds,' Melinda said.

'If we are going to keep my home alive then it is going to require more than just digging holes for others,' and with a finger she stirred the top-soil so the water would seep deep within the pot. Tomorrow I'll find a place to plant these,' and she blew out the candle to fall exhausted to the black of another night.

∞∞∞∞

Ashland looked out to the grey moon, his heart weakened by the memory, young love that was never meant, hers, so right, and when he thought, everything else, so wrong. Grandfather's stories filling his mind like beams of candy wrapped in a croaky voice. "See child that green moon. That's our future. The riches one can make.

The growth of our planet can be fertilized so not one species will go without and when the time is right, you will be our Ambassador." How wrong he was, Ashland thought.

He walked in through the grand doors of a once proud castle and down the stone staircase. Echoes of each footstep his sole companion, beyond a daughter waited. She looked up, walled by books she had never read. Today was the day she would actually read one.

'The grand library holds the past like a philosopher telling a story, some true, some not, but there is knowledge here; mark my words, it is for you to discern the truth Tandiette.' His words absorbing into the century old pages.

'Is discern like concern?'

'No, more like a question.'

'Well father can you explain how, the Unworthy captured mother. You never would say?'

'They didn't capture her, she went back of her own free will, because her moon needed someone to fight for its right. A leader. A Royal.'

'Like a princess?'

'A future queen, yes… I should have never let her go… but once she had a mind to… Tandiette… Royalty is a thing of the past.'

'Like these books, but not mother.'

'Of course, not mother,' and he wondered if he was convincing his daughter or himself.

'I have another question. About the Unworthy…'∞∞∞∞

Chapter 5

Devil Beware

'Teardrops of stewed grunion, I smell the blood of a new Youngling.'

Trapped between two oversized claws of what were once hands, the flicker of the Unworthy's fire sought out a look of terror on a tiny face. A squeal, then out from a rough built hut a leader emerged.

'None of your kin can hear you, we own your country.'

The Youngling kicked and sank two sharp teeth into a claw… Result, the grasp of his captor weakened for a moment, then… the crisp dizzy rush of air on a Youngling rising to the sting of teeth sinking deep into his soft neck. 'You are going to show us the way,' and the beast swallowed. 'I taste the fear squirming with a need to escape.' The Youngling squealed and kicked again until a hand rendered him unconscious and he was dropped like a piece of fresh meat to the ground.

'Devlin,' his leader turned and snarled, 'I mean Master… can't we just eat him? He won't tell us anything of worth.'

Devlin didn't know why he kept the nous of self with the changes, unlike most, who lost themselves to the inviting affliction, but above all he could taste his sense of greed growing with every colony they overwhelmed. 'No, we shall keep him until his need to feed is such that he will have to return to his home world, and if you oafs can manage your taste buds, we might just discover a way into that rock without blunting all our drills.'

The Youngling awoke, hands tied behind his back. The stones of the fire, cold, sun breaking to a brisk dawn. He rolled to his right and sneezed, his smell as rotten as a grislin on a road-trip. The reason he was here in the first place. He thought of how sick his father was, and a mother's words fresh to mind, with hope, an Alderberry root. He squirmed and felt the knot weaken. Was luck on his side? He wished, and the point of his ears spiked as he wrestled with all his strength... Was that a noise in the bushes? Again, he tried and without a sound he pulled his hands free. He scanned the encampment... empty... and if he wasn't struck with the same affliction his father was fast succumbing to, he would be able to smell them a mile away as he sneezed again to no avail. His sack of Alderberry root scattered all over the camp. He quietly collected what he could and stuffed them in the sack... then stopped to listen... Nothing, and without another thought he ran, knowing no oaf could catch him in the thick undergrowth once he made it out of the palm oil shrubs.

'Shh,' from behind the bushes.

'Shouldn't we go after, the Youngling, we might lose the scent?'

Devlin's canines sparkled in the morning dew, 'I have a secret weapon,' and he whistled. The wild thing bristled with spikes, to a foul noxious screech. Devlin held the torn shirt to the Kretin's nose. Nostrils flared and on two hind legs it reared, ready. 'Hold the reins,' Devlin handing them to his second in command and threw a blanket over Destructors back. 'You two mount up.'

'Us, why us?'

Devlin knew they were expendable, but if they could find a sniff of an entrance he would have his reward. 'We can't keep up with Destructor, but her tracks, unmistakable, so I choose you two,' he snarled, a full foot taller than any. For he was one of the first, his power growing deep inside like an unstoppable rage.

They mounted, her snorts excited, eye to eye with her master. He released his grip and wacked her rump, quickly regretted though, spikes burning deep into his hand, and as he looked up, dust erupted to the sound of scrub-trampling hoofs.

'Bloody hell, I hope this blanket is thick enough,' Jebb groaned to Raval who was too busy trying to hang onto the reigns.

'Ten miles feels like one,' Raval replied as a cave entrance loomed large. Too large and Destructor slowed. 'Size matters,' he said to a lump of rock with his name on it and pulled the reigns back hard, as if he thought he was in control, but Destructor bore on, unwanted fleas scratched off by this mammoth. Bruised they picked themselves up to see the light dimming ahead to a background glow of bugs and moss, which they knew none of.

'Light my torch Jebb?'

'Light your own torch,' with footprints fast disappearing to a rock floor as they came to a halt with the tunnel divided into three. 'Here,' Jebb's claws running over the furrowed grooves of the Kreton.' They followed the tunnel ever smaller. Ahead, stuck, Destructor groaned a sooky sound. 'We need to unplug this overgrown mutant, otherwise Master…' and they both grumbled to the thought. He crawled under her belly, careful not to catch a painful spike on the way. 'How are we going to do this Raval,'standing in front of a spiky snout?

'You push and I'll pull her tail.'

Jebb placed his claw-like hands on the only place free of spikes, her snout, and yelled 'Pull!' One foot of Destructor lifted and kicked. Raval flew ten feet and slammed into the curve of the tunnel. A pleasing sound to a Kreton, but she was free as Raval gasped for breath. Together they backed her around to face the correct way out. 'This is as far as you go, beasty,' he said.

They turned and set off into the darkness, the flame of their torches flickering, near burnt out. The tunnel walls closing in. Crawling on all fours the flames flickered and died.

'Now what,' Raval said.

'Up ahead, look.' A pinpoint of light shone. Jebb being the smaller squeezed his body to the opening and looked out. Vegetation erupted from every crevice, but in front, a well-worn track invited. They squeezed through. Above, a translucent ceiling moved with uncertainty. The barrier stopped what looked like an ocean of water. Swirls of currents moved to soften the streams of light. A light breeze fom the tunnel's entrance pushing them in the backs like the underworld had the knowledge of lungs… To cough, or not to cough.

Raval jabbed Jebb in the ribs and whispered, 'Ahead.' The Youngling sprinted and disappeared, hidden in the thick vegetation, only to repeat the process. 'Let's just grab him next time he appears. Enough of this half-foolery.'

'No, we don't know if this is the way in, or not, and remember what happened last time.' He rubbed the still painful black bruise Devlin had left. They moved forward in a vain attempt to replicate the Youngling's efforts, however their affliction made them anything but gracious. The Youngling's ears spiked as he squealed and bolted for an opening on the far side of the rock wall, to disappear, gone.

'See I told you, a weakling in the hand.'

'Come on,' and they ran with no concern of what lay in wait.

What, a snake in the grass? No something larger… as a long tail swirled with half grown wings to sink his jaws into an unwitting Unworthy… Tossed rotating ragged in the moist damp air Jebb spun, before being bit down on and swallowed whole, except for the claws of a left foot that fell stained to one side. Biscuit burped and thought, "At last, something tasty." ∞∞∞∞

Chapter 6

Smoke rings of a different kind

Claritine settled next to her twins. 'Now Tandiette, take note how the twins pronounce their words.'

'What is wrong with my words,' Tandiette replied.

'You have a derelict dialect that has no place in influencing Roselyn and Reisel. In future please refrain from speaking to them direct. You shall go through me, so as to avoid your awful use of language; and please, I mean please, use some moisturizer or something on that sickly skin. I mean to say they might catch something.' Tandiette screwed her face to almost unrecognizable.

'Talking about catching something,' Parian walking in. 'Have you heard the Brewer family are all sick with a flue, or something.

'Another lot of Halflings to avoid, if you ask me,' Claritine said.

'That's not the half of it,' Parian continued. 'Tobian snuck out to fetch the Alderberry root treatment…'

'He disrespected the Dearling Elder's strict order of, "No one leave the caves without permission." Cover your ears twins, and you Parian, shouldn't be spreading rumours.'

'It is not a rumour, and I won't say what he said next.'

'Go away with you. You're probably infectious as well.'

Parian left as Tandiette ran to catch up. 'He went above ground into the open?'

'Yes and... no, he made me promise to say nothing, given...'

'He's put us all at risk, you must.'

'The only thing he would say is he thought he was followed.'

'Followed, by who?'

Parian looked around. 'The Unworthy, but before you go, going off, he said they were eaten by a monster, a very big monster, living in the wastelands.'

'The wastelands... Oh Biscuit... he could be in trouble? We have to check, right now. See I leave you to look after him for two weeks and, and...'

'Calm down, he doesn't need feeding by hand anymore, he grazes at will and I'm sure he knows to keep himself hidden.'

And as they ran, she stopped for a second, 'Father needs to be told.'

'He's in a meeting with the Elders,' Parian replied.

'Right, when we return then,' and she began to run. They held their breath as they passed through the barrier of light. The track ahead littered with broken twigs and vines. 'What's this?' she said.

'Must be the monster Tobian mentioned. Careful Tandiette it might still be lurking,' and he sniffed the air... 'Nothing.'

Carefully they followed the path and stopped at Biscuit's cave entrance. Parian sucked in a deep breath to call his name, but Tandiette's hand was too quick, and trapped with a few squeaks escaping, as she whispered,

'Biscuit are you here?' A growl emerged deep from within the cave, 'I'm going in,' she said.

'Fine leave me out here, to be eaten by who knows what, still, could be worse, I could be a unicorn in a glue factory.'

'Shh,' Tandiette entered and as her eyes adjusted, she saw a huge shape move. A long tongue reached up her arm and down the hollow of her back. 'Oh Biscuit... My... how you've grown, and what a stinky breath you have. What have you been eating?'

Biscuit moved to dwarf his childlike foster mother from another time. He coughed and groaned, 'I feel your pain.'

'What? Who said that?' Tandiette looking everywhere, but the one direction the voice really came from, for she knew that would be impossible.

'Am I all that impossible?' Tandiette pupils dilated, and for the first time she saw her dragon in all his glory. 'Don't be surprised, voice is as old as time,' Biscuit said in a deep scratchy note, tried for this opening occasion.

She stared, and said, 'I never knew. All the things we said and did. You understood them?'

'I understand the feelings we share for each other. What is said, is but words whistling in the wind for a dragon to munch on.'

'I can't wait to show father.'

'A gift shared is easily spoiled. The less others know... but I am your father's humble servant of course.' Tandiette brimmed, emotion building with what they would discuss; what she could learn from her dragon's mouth, not a book full of lies.

'What's going on in here, I thought I heard voices?'

'Parian I have…' and before she could utter a word Biscuit breathed out a fire of sooty smoke, so thick, Parian disappeared; gobbled up in a black mist, where all he could do was head for the exit, coughing.

'That's better,' Biscuit said.

'Why have I this distinct feeling, you want to keep this between you and me,' Biscuit's perfectly round smoke rings, a definite sign.

'I have to go,' Tandiette said. 'I just wanted to know you were safe. There are things afoot. You haven't seen a horrid large creature that wants to eat us lurking about, have you?'

Biscuit burped and said, 'Excuse me, some of what I've eaten lately has left an aftertaste that lingers,' and as if he was considering, he paused and said, 'Nothing of that description.'

'Good, now be careful and stay hidden. There could be danger heading our way.'

'Tandiette are you ready,' Parian impatient as she stroked Biscuits long snout then turned and left with even more questions. Parian stood waiting, looking up to the barrier of light holding back an ocean as he said,

'Tandiette, it's hard, never to go above. I understand we chose to live below for safety, but I miss the fresh clear air, the wide-open spaces, where once, we could be ourselves to relax without a care… and not be eaten.'

∞∞∞∞

Smoke rings of a different kind

Chapter 7

Be careful who we wish for

'Halfway between Virgon and Dearling City, we change to be Imperial my pretty.'

The Arogon's beak twisted to suck in another smell of her master's many faces. Feathered wings flapped another beat before the descent... Down, down, down, through the clouds of ash before breaking free to open air and the latest encampment.

'My Lord.' His Lordling dressed in a dark flowing robe, turned, two piercing black eyes stared deep with a southern chill knowing which part of their bones to ache.

'You tell me of this creature, most foul, that eats us in one gulp?'

Devlin jabbed Raval, 'Go on tell our Lord and master.'

Raval half stepped, half pushed. 'It was huge with big red eyes and blew smoke like our drills on the grey moon. Poor Jebb, he didn't stand a chance. I told him, but he didn't listen... not to show ourselves.'

'And?'

'All I saw was a huge mouth, bristling with teeth, grab him and throw him up into the mist, to be twirled like a dead bat, before,' Raval stopped and looked at the other Unworthy faces.

'Before what?'

'He was swallowed whole.'

'What sort of creature was this beast, able to swallow one of us whole?'

'Never seen anything like it in my life.'

'Your life,' and he twirled his cane and the magic rose the hairs on Raval's head to greet the blue flame, cut down to bare root, naked, with only his words to protect him.

'I can show the way, I can, I can, oh great and powerful Lord,' as he knelt before his Lordling.

'Hmm, Devlin we have that lumbering ox you call the Kretin don't we, he knows the way, doesn't he?'

'But, but... I saw where the Halfling went, I did, I did,' Raval pleaded.

The Lordling's flowing robe swung out, a cape of fear as his cane spun in his hand, practised by need, and he holstered the weapon into the studded scabbard.

'My Pretty,' he said as the Arogon swooped low to land, its wings tucked back so he could mount, claws the size of a Halfling, digging deep into the dirt. He leaned into Devlin's ear and said, 'Raval is our clue, make sure he stays safe, and no Unworthy is to enter the Dearling City without my order, or you will feel the full force of my mistress.' He lay his hand on the weapon so there would be no mistake.

'Of course, my Lord,' Devlin said before he shielded his face from the flap of wing and rush of turbulence.

They rose high on a current of ash. Virgon a mere two hours. The volcano's ash gave way to the mist of clouds until even they were left below. The air clean between the worlds, rivers of untamed currents sweeping to doom

44

unless one had a creature wise to the crossing, his thoughts wrestled wild on events as he whispered, 'My pretty.' Her feathers ruffled as he let loose her reins, instinct her ruler. Time a meaningless necessity when all his plans were in place, except for one. The Arogon's wings flapped high over Virgon's royal castle, ready to swoop down and nestle behind a mountain... The Lordling dismantled, 'Here my pretty,' he held out a handful of grain. She squawked to his touch as he pulled her headdress firm over both eyes. To the left the stone-house, windows broken long ago as he led the Arogon to the rear of the building. 'Stay, my pretty, stay.' She cooed to his soft touch and change of voice, safe in her stable. The back door's rusty hinges creaked as he turned the old lock and entered.

Inside he disrobed and carefully removed the glowing blue jewel from his cane, only to replace it with a fake. Clear of eye he stared at the changing shape of his reflection, as real as a zirconium in the crown jewels. The air stale as he entered the secret passage, winding down he went, like a never-ending cold contusion safely tucked into the shine of the fakery of his light. He stopped and looked out. The view limited by the deceptiveness of the peephole. So, he stayed hidden for a while. Quiet his friend as the hidden entrance swung open and he walked through to close what will be unnoticed, a shelf of normal, but caught by his cane, a book fell... "Thud" and he nearly dropped his aid.

'Is someone there?' Tandiette said. She rose from the table of books her father had handpicked and walked between the aisle shelves dwarfing her, near the end. He hobbled, walking stick in hand when she saw him. 'Do you need a hand Sir Erin, I didn't hear you enter.'

'No, my child. You are Ashland's servant girl, aren't you?'

'Yes, I was…am… as you can see, he is teaching me to read, and well, without much success, I'm afraid.'

'Don't let me stop you, I have my cane,' and he leant heavily on the glass crystal at its head. 'Age my dearie is a very unforgiving mistress,' and he waited for Tandiette to walk back to her table before he entered the secret room, dead ahead.

'It's about time Erin old boy, we've nearly given up on you,' William said.

'So, what is this all about?'

'Ashland has news of his Seraphina.'

'You have?' Tell me I'm all ears,' and he coughed like age was willed by his chameleon of another creature.

'Are you all right, that cough sounds awful,' Ashland said.

'I'm fine. Go on,' he replied.

'A rescue, no less' and Sir Erin coughed again, this time like he choked down something that had no place surfacing. ∞∞∞∞

Chapter 8

The boy

Ashland stared across the fields. Dreams of what was filled his mind. They walked on, Tandiette step for step. Ahead, the paddocks of wheat harvested by hand, workers barely stopping to look as they trod amongst them, boots sinking into the freshly ploughed furrow. An oxen's broken breath intent with recovery and the shaking of its reign. 'This way Tandiette,' Ashland pointing to the village ahead.

They stepped cautiously onto the wooden planks and scraped the mud from their boots. The Village no more than a main street with two shops and an Alchemist at the end. 'This one,' Ashland said. Stale food moved, as they stepped to startled weevils and mice on the twisted wooden shelves. At the rear, a shadowy figure rustled.

'We are closed for the harvest,' she said.

'Tell the Raven we are here to ask a favour,' Ashland said.

'The Raven. I haven't heard that name spoken in decades,' she said taking a hair pin and tying down a dangling piece. 'Who speaks that name?' her stare all consuming.

'I do, the Fox,' Ashland replied, and Tandiette just looked at her father because she knew none of this. Then...

'Ashland is that you, it can't be, and who have we here... Oh...' and she walked around Tandiette as if she was studying every feature. 'So much like your mother,' she said.

'Who are you?' Ashland said.

'Remember the rain and the game, a Fox and a Raven would play. Who were you trying to fool, maybe the foolish little girl that fell for every gullible trick, hmm?'

'Melissa, it can't be?'

'As real as your little girl standing in front of me,' and Tandiette screwed her face.

'Look at you, all grown up,' Ashland said.

'More grown old before my time with what's happened,' and her forehead wrinkled to lines of worry. 'Tom's in the fields. I'm surprised you didn't pass him when you entered.'

'He did,' a deep voice echoed from the store's rocky facade, but before he entered he stood aside for another to lower his head and enter first. 'Meet the Glute,' Tom said. They stared, his hands the size of wheat bags as he came to rest, head and shoulders above Ashland. Tandiette's senses bristling with skin blistering to silver. 'Don't worry my dearie, he's not an Unworthy. There were giants long before the disease we call, The Unworthy, took hold.'

'We've found Seraphina,' Ashland's impatience growing. 'The message said she is in pretty bad shape and if we don't go soon... well, that's why we are here, to hatch a plan.'

'You know they've taken any full grown Arogons capable of the journey, don't you, unless you know something we don't?' Tom said.

Ashland smiled at him. 'We have something else up our sleeves, don't we Tandiette?'

Tandiette shook her head and said, 'He's not ready.'

'I was talking about Ismelda.'

'Oh, the two of us?'

'How does anyone receive news from the grey moon, it is like being touched by death itself; all we see are the devils themselves fly in on those Arogon creatures, ready to pluck us like thieves in the night, and our kin, never seen again, that was until we had help. Isn't that right Glute?' and she rested her hand on a massive forearm.

'Glute protect, Glute does.'

'Yes Glute and we appreciate every one of those beasts you slay.' and he swung his massive frame to look down on Melissa, but alas two shelves gave way like tooth picks with musky rodents playing three blind mice.on his hand.

'Glute clumsy, so clumsy.'

'No Glute you are beautiful,' she said, and his smile so wide they could feel the gasps of the Unworthy's fright between his molars.

'Ravens,' Ashland said. 'Someone is sending messengers on Ravens and I have a good idea who.'

'Go on,' Melissa said.

'No one else could train birds like she could. A pigeon in another's hand, a raven in hers. She has a way only a daughter can better,' and Tandiette smiled, her first in a very long time. 'We aim to go and get her, come rain and hot ash, isn't that right Tandiette?'

'Too damn right,' she said.

'What we need is an exact location these messages were sent from?'

'How are we to know that?' Tom said. 'Take a look around, do we look as if we could help rescue anyone, even your beloved Seraphina. You know as well as me, anyone setting foot on that damned moon runs the risk of turning into one of those freaks. How can you be sure she hasn't already, god forbid, and this is just a trap, for you, our one true ruler, Ashland?'

'Because she sent something else, something that couldn't be carried by a raven, something that can turn the tide and save us all. Someone here within this very village received that gift and they know her location, I'm sure of it.'

'Who, tell us who? Tom said.

Tandiette saw a familiar face staring through the shop's bay window. She tugged on her father's arm and said, 'Father, may I go outside, don't you see,' and his gaze followed hers, without an answer to the question.

'Fine,' he said, 'but don't be long, the daylight's getting away.'

Tandiette left the conversation to the adults and ventured out to see if he was real.

'Servant girl,' as he looked up and down to see what had changed. 'Here we are, a thief and his protector?'

'I'm not your protector,' Tandiette said.

'Answer me this then… Why a master, with so much influence, and much more that doesn't meet the eye, visit us, here?'

'Why not, says me, and you question… A thief with too many secrets and an eye for everyone. I know you know, so tell me,' and she gave him the face, saved for special occasions and asked. 'Where will we find the one who received "the gift" from the grey moon?'

He looked at her sideways, because he had seen that face before, 'Come with me,' he said, as they walked past the field workers to the soft track reaching into the mountains. Far off, a windglass shied to pricked ears and they saw two grand horns trained on them. 'Stay close, no sudden jerks… as one. Such a magnificent creature, sad what others do with the horns…' and the wild thing lowered its eyes to the grass once more. He looked down and felt each one of his four fingers with his thumb, as if what he had to say, was an effort, 'So who are you really?'

'Ha, ha, you are funny, my little jailor's toy…Why?'

'I have eyes and a nose, I saw when the jailor lifted the beany, worn so carefully pulled down. You are not from around here, are you?'

'If I show you, you must promise to keep my secret,' and she looked back to see they were out of sight. 'My father's and mother's life depend on this,' and she spat on the palm of her hand for the meaning of the oath to be kept. Without being asked, he did the same, and they shook. 'So you know the oath of thieves and what it means?'

'Yes,' and she carefully lifted her beany to reveal her ears, naked as a Halfling can be on a sticky track of another world. 'I knew it,' he said, 'but remember Tandiette not all Halflings have pointed ears,' and he smiled.

'What?'

'A full-grown Halfling on one world, a boy on another, who would ever know.'

'But how?

'Your father brought us all here when the Unworthy overwhelmed the stronghold of Leverton on our world. No one ever thought that would happen, long before the Dearling escaped underground, but here this was a perfect hiding place, indistinguishable to a full blown Tidan except the one aspect we share Tandiette, size.'

She stood eye to eye with him and said, 'I still don't know your name?'

'Radian... Come, I have something to show you.' The track rose up and over the first hill to settle in a lush valley. Two fingers divided his lips as a shrill whistle escaped. High above she saw the spec, almost a sparrow the way it spun, comets of tail feathers straining, growing beyond a deadly shadow blocking the sun, wings twelve feet across opening. It landed next to him. 'Just another egg I had the privilege to squirrel away from those devils,' and he stroked the Arogon, a surrogate father to an overgrown chick, squawking endearments on his every touch.

Tandiette's eyes widened, seeing for the first time, 'Have you seen my mother, have you?' saucers turning to slithers of what he knew.

'I don't know. I flew to that place in search of my family, avoiding those devils was near an impossibility, but like every crowd, a thief knows how to mingle, a rodent amongst many, and that's when the word was whispered of a find, unlike no other... They had found, where dragons go to die... with every one of my questions I ran the risk.' He shook his head and lifted his hand to his Arogon's lowered neck and he stroked the bird again. 'Whoever she was, she held a reverence in the filth of that place. Her words like reasons to try again in my search for a brother and sister.'

'What words?'

'Take this to Ashland, Radian,' and she knew my name like I was a little lost boy, found.'

'We have to tell my father. The information you hold, has to be the answer.'

He smiled and said, 'You speak the tongue of your mother like I speak the tongue of my father,' and he let a tear fall before he turned away.

'Your father, who was your father?'

He paused, 'Gone, like so many who ran foul to the deadly dust. They say those who turn hold too many sins to fight the curse, but I refuse to believe. I have breathed the dust and, look, still as ugly as sin.'

'You're not ugly,' her face flushed with a new emotion. ∞∞∞∞

The Last Dragon's egg

Chapter 9

The grey moon

'I don't think your Arogon likes Ismelda?' Tandiette said as the bird lifted her beak to defend an unwanted jab from the sharp toothed Ductile.

'Jessie can be temperamental, but once in the air she is as graceful as an eagle,' Radian replied.

'So how far is the camp?' Ashland said.

'Three miles,' tying his scarf above his nose. 'I suggest you do the same, the dust is deadly in more ways than one.'

'Only to those who are of mean spirit,' Tandiette said. 'But still,' and she pulled two cotton handkerchiefs, one for her and one for her father.

'Bandits we three, about to pull off the abduction of the decade,' Radian said, his smile masked, because they all knew this was no laughing matter. 'Careful, by foot, there are mine holes filled by the dust, impossible to see, that's why no Unworthy will be caught dead walking here. These mounds are the tailings,' and with a wave of his hand a cloud of fine grey particles followed.

'Father you said the moon's soil is rich in nutrients, but, by the likes of these,' and she pointed to a drift twenty feet high, sifted so fine, their footsteps disturbed clouds growing to follow like evil spirits ready to betray.

'I did,' he replied, mind busy with other matters.

'What's the difference between a crow and a raven,' Radian said.

'Is that a trick question?' Tandiette said.

'No.'

'Depends on which world you are from. A raven on one, a crow on another,' Ashland said.

'Like an Unworthy, from last time. Able to transform from terrible to troubling.'

'Would you recognize the creature again?' Ashland said, puzzled.

'Oh yes, every ugly feature,' and he turned off the track. 'We need to follow from unwanted eyes from here.' He pointed to a crack in the ground, a squeeze for all. 'Leave our transport here,' as he tied his to a rock. 'Stay my friend, stay,' he said.

Tandiette did the same, but all she needed was her reddened eyes for Ismelda to understand, a mistress from another world, as it rested on the grey dirt, mouth closed.

Ahead, streams of light filtered by stalactites, crystalline jewels falling, disappearing into the depths of darkness.

'The cave where dragons go to die,' Radian said and he pulled a flint to strike the near burnt out torch from a wall, flints tempered by the flame's struggle, near on refusing his will. Tandiette leaned close and blew as one with him. 'Not all can see in the dark like Dearlings.'

Tandiette smiled... 'We may surprise you Radian, isn't that right father?'

'Better we are sure of foot, this place looks ancient,' as her father's foot broke a rock that plummeted off the edge into the black void, and they waited without the sound of bottom.

Deeper they walked, drips of water dribbling over Radian's face and he stopped. 'Right here, I remember her words. "What you see above doesn't reflect, in any way, my world. Once, the green grass of home, where liquid fell like dreams, tears of our mother's moon, torn away by,' and with her words he sighed, "the demon greed of Tidans," and I agreed, boy, did I agree. She then went on to say, it hadn't rained in four years, clouds nothing but mist on the horizon.'

Ashland swallowed hard, 'We have a lot to answer for,' and they walked on.

Radian stopped again and lit the remnant of another torch, only to see the flicker washed with the bony grey face of a monster.

'Oh dear, the poor thing, I wonder how long ago it died?' Tandiette said.

'Hard to say, a century, a millennium, one could never know preserved like it is in this underground tomb.'

The bony skull of a head looked down on Tandiette, as she passed, with body and tail crumbling to an end in the distance. 'I think we'll need a bigger cave for Biscuit,' she said.

'Who's Biscuit?' Radian said.

'A food group of a different sort,' Ashland replied.

'Father!'

'Come on… How much further, Radian?'

'Another ten minutes, maybe less,' he said. Jaw bones to sunken eye sockets glared all about like statues to the gods. 'She said this was where she found the egg. A rock she thought, but when she cast it down, the dust of time fell away to expose a glimmer of silver. And that's not all she said. *A leader found his power here, long before the disease took hold.*'

57

'What leader? Did she give a name?'

'No, she wouldn't. Too dangerous she said. For everyone.' They stopped and looked up through the ceiling of rock, threads of light showed them they were close. 'The slaves,' and he saw Tandiette's face flicker to a disturbing distortion... 'I mean captives... they worked the cave ahead, last time, so tread carefully and be ready to hide.' Radian stopped behind the bend and doused his torch, then Tandiette's. Peering out of the darkness light streamed down, almost blinding, so pure, not even a breath of dust was disturbed. 'They must have moved on, the real soil exhausted; as you would know Sir Ashland, as rich as gold to the right person on Tidan.'

'Come on, we're not here for treasure, boy,' Ashland said.

'Carefully though, just one of those Unworthy is a match for Glute, two and he's likely to be missing some teeth.'

'Let me at them, those monsters, I'll show them they can't take my mother.'

'Tandiette... no... stealth is our friend,' as Ashland slid his studded dagger back in the scabbard and out of the cave they crept.

'The camps over the hill,' Radian pointing as they scampered rock to rock, but all they saw was empty sky, not a sign of life, like a dead world. Hidden, they peered down. The shadowy footprint of a camp below, barbed thatched wooden fencing torn down, all that remained standing, two primitive huts. 'They've gone,' Radian said as they waited for a sign of something.

'Enough, show me where she slept,' Ashland demanded.

Down they went stepping over the leftovers of a perimeter fence to where previously, each tent stood, outlined only by the build-up of dust. 'This was hers, I think. Hard to tell now.'

Ashland fossicked with a boot through the site to an edge where two green buds glistened to a lost remnant of life. He bent down and blew the grey dust from the roots. 'Freshly planted,' he said. 'She was here. No one else cared like my Seraphina for this world. No one.'

'We will catch up. They leave a trail a mile wide,' Tandiette said.

'Maybe, but this is a whole new scenario,' Ashland said. 'They'll be guarded, on the lookout, with who knows how many.'

'We have to try,' Tandiette pleaded.

'I know how you feel about your mother, but the first sign of her, and,' he stopped and looked into his daughter's eyes. 'I don't want to lose you both,' as he turned his gaze to the distant mountains of Volantrium. Wiping his moist nose, ragged peaks wandered on a tear, climbing ten-thousand feet or more, he thought... a perfect spot for an ambush, but by whom?

'We don't even know how far their lead is,' Radian said, as Tandiette's nostrils flared.

'Did you smell that,' she said.

'No,' Radian replied, and they walked as the path narrowed to disappear into a towering gorge, dead ahead.

'What smell Tandiette,' Ashland asked, nose to the air.

'The rancid taste of,' her mouth filled with deathly silence.

'I don't trust this place, it could be an ambush,' Ashland said.

'That's only if they know we were coming, surely?' Radian said.

'Surely, but just the same,' Ashland's nose twitched by past failures and the rocky ridges that blocked his choice on both sides of the track.

'What, climb that,' Radian said.

'It'll give us a vantage point to look down and see our dangers.'

'Or fall and get killed just the same,' Radian said smiling, for any thief worth his salt could scale a castle's face like a lizard in the dark...

Radian looked back down, Tandiette so close he could feel her hot breath on his neck. Ashland left hanging halfway, struggling with footholds and a face of determination, and so they climbed on until every rock meant another one waited... 'Over here Radian whispered,' finger to lip and an eye that said look. Below, two guards, and spreading out, three hundred threadbare captives troubled by tents that were piled high on broken wagons. The Oxen snouts deep in the broken bales of hay. Tandiette's eyes strained to see a loved one, as Radian gestured to Ashland who was struggling over the last peak. Breathless, Ashland sucked in the mountain air and wiped his frown to a sitting position next to his daughter.

Tandiette whispered, 'Can you see her?'

'Give me a moment,' and he wiped his face again and looked.

'Mother would have changed, I don't even know if I would know her now,' and Tandiette tried to imagine her mother from when she was that little girl. 'Maybe her voice, maybe her smell.'

'I see them,' Radian near exploding, and one guard looked in their direction, before his claw scratched his rope matted hair.

'Do you see my mother?'

'I see my brother and sister, in with the children. See over to the rear of that wagon,' and he pointed.

'Careful, these beasts may be clumsy, but when it comes to instincts, they are wild animals,' Ashland said clinging to the sinews of bare rock. 'We have to wait before daring another look.' With the moments pressing he lifted his head to stare intensely at, each and every one, of the three hundred. 'She's not there,' slumping back. 'I don't understand, every sign, points to her being here. What am I missing,' and he had a horrid thought he dare not tell Tandiette, the bodies of the ones left behind, piled downwind.

'Mother or no mother, I'm going in,' Radian said. 'I haven't come this far to turn back.' He looked at the shadows creeping ever longer, 'In an hour, darkness falls, and those creatures are as blind as Tidans during an eclipse.

'No, you will be spotted, wait for the dark,' Ashland said.

'Dark smark, this Youngling is quicker and smarter than anyone of them, and I don't want to lose Tara and William in the dark of tent city going up.'

'Careful Radian, and remember, just remember you're my little thief,' Tandiette whispered.

'Anyone would have thought you cared,' and he smiled.

'You are your own person Radian and I thank you for all your help, but this is madness. All I can say, is wait, there is always another way.'

'Sorry Sir Ashland,' and down he crept, skirting behind the peaks. The sparse vegetation that grew out of the Unworthy's reach were flowers of another kind for his cunning and no one would have a clue from the campsite.

Tandiette was the first to spot it. Low down like a speck of dirt, hiding in the setting sun. The flap of wing tuned to an unmistakable beat. She stared for a moment hoping the mirage was a ghost of the mind, but as the image grew to her sinking heart, she turned to her father, 'We have to warn Radian,' she whispered.

'How? Any move we make will only alert them to his presence. No, stay put and hope whatever's riding that Arogon doesn't spot him, or us.'

Tandiette sucked in her silent gasp to the creature's circle. A bead of eyes overhead as they climbed high over the encampment. She watched as Radian moved near the tents, to nestle in a shrub, hardly moving, and she prayed he would look up. Without a sound he moved and what befell her eyes made her leak sobs to the winged creature wired to Radian's every motion, and the Arogon swooped. A rider's rein loose to lean into the dive, almost majestic to an untrained eye, but she knew what an Arogon can do with a claw. Parian ripped shrub and all into the air, and like any animal, dropped twenty feet to the ground. Prey broken, barely moving, as the bird and his beast-master nestled next to the startled children and their once free brother. ∞∞∞∞

Chapter 10

Finding our place

Echoes across the square, a little Youngling sang to all the lost; desperate words to dark times…

'Far be gone, father of mine
Be my memory, be back in time
Never be a devil, never be some Unworthy thing…'

'Reach into my pocket and grab my time piece,' Ashland said, hands full with offerings and they walked on, then, a deep breath as they passed through the light barrier, a path once overgrown, charred both sides.

Parian waited at the end of the winding trail, hands on hips. 'About time,' he said.
'So, how's my Biscuit,' Tandiette asked, her Dearling words twisted strange by a mouthful of traumatic turns, without a single deed to washaway the sins.
'We've moved, you'll see.' They followed the scorched ground to a large opening in the rocks. Three bats circled, all that told, their squeaks behind the dark curtain. 'We need a safe word,' Parian said.
'Why?'

'You'll see sis,' their father struggling ten feet behind, arms full. Parian yelled, 'We're here Biscuit...'his pointy ears tuned, twitching for a response.

'Why are we waiting, what's the big deal?' Tandiette said, and before she could ask another question, she felt the rough moist texture of her baby's tongue tasting her face. 'Oh, how you've grown,' his head poking out of the gloom into the light of the underworld. Their father stopped in his tracks and dropped his treats and looked up to the marvel of a near full grown dragon.

Biscuit turned his head away and coughed out a black puff before taking a full breath, as if to control something, then he breathed out the pure energy of a dragon's breath with the surrounding jungle exploding into a curtain of flame. They gasped and stepped back, held hard against the rock by the wall of heat. Biscuit walked out to spread his wings and by the light of the flames he stretched his silhouette to rise like a prehistoric legend disappearing in the smoke of his own making. A thousand feet above, no less, he held the light barrier open for a second and an ocean's drop poured on the burning bush, with all that was, evaporated, in the water-soaked charred remnant of vegetation, and with a puff of wet jowls he landed.

'See that's why,' Parian said. Biscuit looked at each of them and bowed his head as if to say sorry. 'Truly amazing, but scary, don't you think,' Parian said.

'I've heard stories, but never believed,' Ashland said with Biscuit bowed before him, then, Biscuit stood tall to clear his throat again, and they ran for the cave this time, just in case; however all that emanated was the deep croak of a full voice.

'Forgive me, I am but a young one, with all the failings and needs,' as he licked his large lips and stared directly at Ashland's treats abandoned to the charred dirt.

'He speaks!' Ashland's mouth unable to close fully, turning to Tandiette ... 'He talks?'

'Yes father, he talks. We didn't want to worry you with his progress given...' and she held back, for to say more would only end in tears and how would that look to her big baby testing the packaging of Ashland's delights.

'Sorry, my mother's father, but may I indulge,' Biscuit croaked.

In disbelief Ashland said, 'Of course,' and with that Biscuit tossed the package into the air and opened his mouth to catch and chew like an oversized lolly, only to cease and spit the wrapping against the rock wall, before biting delightfully, then suck, savouring the taste, before swallowing all that remained.

'Ah,' he burped, 'some animals are tastier than others.'

'Father, I hope you put some greens with that?'

'Everything you had ordered, my daughter... So formal training, I have a book,' and he looked at Biscuit, whose tail waged twenty feet of jungle flat... 'We may need some help?'

'Father... Biscuit,' as she stroked her symbiont's face. 'Explaining this is like trying to say how the moons know which way to turn, but we will work around any problem. To bring strangers here would invite trouble, don't you think?'

'Yea, he might eat them, lightly crisped first though,' Parian said.

'So what do you have in mind, Tandiette?'

'Biscuit and me, can work it out,' and she stroked his face again, 'our relationship... By doing, not some book,

65

hands on, how things were, no fancy pants words. You always said our family ties led direct to a dragons-mind. Let me prove my worth. Let me be the one.'

He looked at Biscuit's massive teeth being picked clean by a long rough tongue and said, 'Hard to believe we have anything in common.'

'Why don't you and Parian leave me and Biscuit to see what we can figure out? Safer that way.'

'Fine by me,' Parian said.

'Are you sure,' Ashland looking at the enormous beast sniffing around to see he hadn't missed any of the treats.

'Father I'll… I mean we'll be fine. You run along and play with those kids of yours.'

'They are related to you as well Tandiette.'

'Whatever, please go, I want to speak to my baby… alone.'

'So much like your mother. Come on Parian, how's that friend of yours with the flue?'

'Alderberry root's a wonder,' and off they went.

'Biscuit,' Tandiette called and he looked up.

'Yes mother,' he growled.

'We have a problem. Bad creatures want to eradicate us, and we need your help to stop them, but first, you must learn to do what I say.'

'You say. Do you believe you are the master of what a dragon thinks or says,' as he scratched his large frame against the rock wall, leaving deep furrows in the loose rubble.

'I feel our connection. Surely you sense it?'

'I am your protector and that of your blood line. Others… I eat others.'

'No, bad dragon. Others are our friends. No eating; understand!'

'What is it about others you like?' Biscuit turned to flattening himself on the ground like an animal pretending to be invisible to prey.

She looked at the large mound and said, 'How can you speak, or even understand all the words we say?'

'There is one thing about dragons. Memory to us is filled with the past, every deed that ever crossed an ancestor. You might say, born with a thousand years of history. A mind so full we only need instinct to dictate our actions. To unlearn is the problem, like not to eat others.'

'Hard to believe we share a common ancestor.'

'We are closer than you realize, mother. What we show on the outside is not what we are on the inside. The light,' and his nose pointed to the ocean swirling above, 'exposes our true feelings, our true meaning. Your skin is your shell and the light will set you free to be what you really are. A thing of beauty, not one thing or another, but one of three worlds with all the mistakes, wealth and magnificence they hold. To return you must cast off all feelings of wrongs and accept yourself for who you really are. Once you can do that, you will be free to be whoever you want. Come climb aboard, let me take you to a place where our minds are one and every thought of mine will be yours.'

Tandiette's nose twitched with the unknown, but she felt his need and without a doubt she climbed Biscuit's back, every scale a stepping-stone to what would come. He opened his wings and flapped and off she spun, face first into the mud. 'Damn,' she said. 'You could have warned me?'

'You fall right off, you get right back, when you do all the crud things. It's not the bruise, it is not the mud, but the love that makes you hang on tight.'

67

'I haven't a brain full of the past, like you. I'm going to make mistakes,' and she wiped her face on her only piece of sleeve not dripping.

'Sorry mother, mistakes are what it takes.'

This time, they rose higher on every flap of wing. Gliding like a serpent skimming below the light barrier as she clung on.

'Raise your head and take a breath,' Biscuit growled.

She froze, embedded with a rule time had forgotten, and said, 'The gods of the Dearlings will cast me out if I dare breath the light. Never to walk in their midst again, an outcast.'

'True you will be different, so changed maybe your kin might reject. I cannot make you be something you don't want to be, I can only show you the way; it is for you to decide.'

Head spinning with the height she said, 'Take me down Biscuit, I think, enough training for today.'

She walked the trail, thoughts without answers, heart saddened with the unknown of her mother's plight. Dark she emerged eyes squinting in the light of Dearling city.

Parian was playing Skiddish-ball, pants torn on the rough surface. 'Come Tandiette, you used to love the game, and I could do with some help?'

A team of five Dearlings stared at her brother and laughed. 'Halflings are as worthless as their useless half-bred parent.' Rabbits painful taunts, nothing new. Normally ignored by Halflings. Tandiette having none of his lip when she saw their cheer squad. The twins dressed by colour as if they belonged, with Claritine shaking the banner, "Dearlings rule."

'Porcupine, you're out, Tandiette's in.'

'Come on,' Porcupine protested, but he knew he had dropped the ball on the last five plays. The ball ran off each time, to a pen of ten, each fed to a prescription. Fat to skinny. Choice all part of the game.

Parian reached in and picked the leanest. Speed, he thought, not always guaranteed and remembered the last group of Skiddish, the rodents now choice, on special, at Crow's feet. Value he knew comes in all sizes. 'Same rules, five aside,' he said to Rabbit.

'Girls need their own team, we play no rules here, Parian.'

'What, you scared of a little girl, Rabbit; scared of being beaten.'

'Fine, but I warned you Halfling,' and pointed to the scoreboard, six one in his favour.

'Ready Tandiette,' she screwed her nose and looked at her stepmother shaking the banner.

'Sure. Let the rodent loose.'

'Tandiette just so you know, the Umps a Quarterling in the Dearling's favour, my protests, useless,' as Parian placed the Skiddish fur ball down into the cage. They waited for it to squeak and unwind its long slim body, with four feet ready to scamper, flat snout pressed firm against the door. 'Experienced little critter, aren't you,' Parian said as the Ump opened the door. Off it ran, darting between legs, however one touch was all a player needed, instinct petrified the critter into a tight fur-ball rolling. Bang! Rabbit sent Parian flying with a full hip and shoulder. The five aside teams both well balanced, but Dearlings were quicker on the turn, however in open space slower than Halflings.

'That's a foul Ump,' Parian groaned, as the Dearlings threw from one to another, before slam dunking into the never ever broken web-net of a Venom spiders entwine.

'Seven one,' Rabbit boasted to the cheer-squad, and the applause of the crowd.

'Here brother,' Tandiette offering a hand for him to stand. 'Let me do the next chase.'

Rabbit chose the fattest, as the Ump raised the door and she smiled at Rabbit, ears straight up, canines sparkled by every light source of the grand arena. The cheer squad chanted, "Dearling's Rule."

Tandiette hadn't played the game in three years, but a child doesn't forgive or forget, as Rabbit's hip bone bore like a rabid ram into her side. She was swept sideways, feet trying to find firm footholds on the rough ground. She smiled again when her skin transformed to a silvery white, eyes of green, as he reached for the fur-ball of rodent his every step shadowed, and when he threw, the rodent was hers, like taking fun from a bully, her heart beat tied to a breath, rotating mid-air and she hadn't realized she'd leapt six feet to intercept. Impossible for any Halfling, only she wasn't any Halfling, she was more. She landed, poised, before the Dearlings knew they had lost the ball. One looked at his hands as if to ask, where?

Parian yelled, 'Pass, I'm free.'

She looked at him and smiled, her enthusiasm peaked with a right arm so quick the Skiddish lost consciousness for a second. Twenty feet was crossed in a milli-moment before hitting the spider's web-net, and the Skiddish slowed tightening every strand of fine thread beyond breaking, the rodent hurtling on to the far side of the cavern piling into a family of Dearlings waiting for rations. The rodent spread like a long fluffy legging, stunned, not moving before letting out an ear-burning squeal, as it ran for the Cavern's exit, gone, never to be seen again.

The Ump blew his whistle. 'Foul,' he called.

'What!' Parian said. 'How can that be a foul, the ball went in the net?'

'Did it stay in the net? No… so the score doesn't count.'

'Doesn't count, what a crock,' Parian mumbled below his breath.

'Next time I'll be gentler,' Tandiette said as she rolled up her sleeves and Parian stared.

'What's wrong with your skin Sis?

She looked down and both arms were erupting like they had been sun burnt a week ago and the layers flacking in scales.

'Oh dear,' she said. 'I should sit the next one out. Sorry Parian,' and she walked toward the twins.

'Oh no you don't,' and Tandiette pulled both sleeves as far down as she could. 'See how ugly your stepsister has grown. Gone to that hideous moon she has. Stay away from us, infectious you can be.'

Tandiette didn't know, all she knew was she was changing, into what, she couldn't say. "Maybe father would know?" She hoped. ∞∞∞∞

Chapter 11

The Golden City

Walls a hundred feet high, so smooth a possum couldn't breathe in the cracks. 'Talk to me father, why here... will we find an answer?'

He looked at the gate. The crest of a dragon sparkled, rich with gold inlays and their four-legged berison rested, tied to the golden railing as they dismounted. 'Remember, servant girl, nothing else.'

She checked her beany, as he produced a golden invitation with his name. Tall towers breathed eyes every fifty feet, crossbows fine strung, stretched, pointing down. Rumoured to be capable of twenty shafts a minute. No guards waited, no need, no way in, but two. They walked to the door as a hatch the size of a face opened. 'Invitation,' Tandiette heard and Ashland handed over his way in. 'A moment,' then, 'Who is the child?'

'A servant,' and the hatch closed, and as they waited, creaks of metal on metal ground unlike any Tandiette had heard before. A slither opened, the experience of an entrance into wonderland.

'Enter,' a voice said. Tandiette looked up, ten feet of metal shone thick, only to dull in the shadow of its own makings. Buildings and antiquities rose in the city of plenty. Roads so smooth she wanted to remove her shoes so her toes could feel the firmness. Precious metals shone from windows and balconies. Residents refined by silken thread and sandals. Rich smells dripped to strange smiles and a sense of self-satisfied confidence.

'Who are we going to see fa... master?'

He looked back to where the gate patrol stood checking guests as they entered. 'We are going to the Ball.'

'Ball, what Ball?' Tandiette no clue.

'Once a year, the Golden City sends out invitations to selected Tidans, to celebrate, with them, the chosen ones.'

'Are you one of the chosen ones?'

He smiled and said, 'If they only knew. Take a look around, all this wealth, all these possessions and when you look beyond, trapped like rats by giant walls; afraid to step one foot out. They need us to make them feel superior, reaffirming what they are doing is right. Beyond the glitter we have to look, that's where the answers lie.'

They walked, following other invitees. The building decorated with a doorman. Inside she held onto her beany when the attendant asked if she wanted to leave her hat, stranger still, a contraption surrounded by a golden cage.

'After you,' her father said. Hesitant she stepped in as he slid the door closed and to her surprise, they rose, like magic in a cage. 'So we don't have to walk the stairs,' he said.

'How?' Through the cracks two floors down, she heard the crank and grunts, and for a moment she thought she saw the movement of a giant's eye.

Her father just smiled again and said, 'Every excess comes at a cost.' Five floors up, the room. Her father pulled a key and unlocked the door. 'Our room,' and Tandiette's nose filled with a dozen smells. Flowers spread throughout, and as she walked into this extravagance a bath stood within a glass cubicle. 'To wash oneself,' and her father turned the tap to show how such a marvel filled.

She smiled and went to the window and looked out at the amazements. Her eyes filled by the wealth of beauty, that was, until her arms began to itch again, and she scratched. This time two full grown scales fell to the ground and she pulled her sleeves down, as if they weren't real.

'Tonight Tandiette, when the music is full and the dancers are engaged, we will slip out to,' and he stroked his chin, 'to experience the unbelievable. For today we eat the fruit and drink the wine.'

'No wine for me, father. Maybe one of those,' and with a mouth filled by a million spices she coughed her first smoke ring.

'Oh daughter, you are a living, walking, miracle.'

She turned away, face burnt by embarrassment and the words of a stepmother. 'Am I turned... am I an ugly freak?' tears slipping down her face, running to sink deep into the silk of a bed's pillow.

Her sobs muffled as her father's hand reached and stroked. His little girl all grown up. 'No, you are our future,' he said.

∞ ∞   ∞

Tandiette's eyes glowed in the dim as she watched the darkness engulf bodies, illuminated shapes caught, glimpsed by a rotating ball of light. Dancers from three worlds, and not one Dearling City invitee that they knew of. They twisted and spun to the "ooh's and ah's" of the gentry. Invitees lined up like trophies, to impress, what the wealth of three worlds could show, she thought.

She stood with the other servants ready to respond to a master's whim. Only when the show ceased did the leader speak. He held his head high, face bronzed, almost without a wrinkle. Oiled so smooth his age lines glistened. Tandiette thought he could turn to bronze and no one would notice, words so smooth, juiced by the palm oil plantation after the Unworthy had swept resistance clean.

She looked to her father who was becoming surrounded by the local female population. She'd never thought of her father in that way before, as couples began to dance and he respectfully declined one after another. How stupid she felt, along with the irony of ugliness creeping like a disease beneath her clothes.

He broke away and headed towards her. 'We must go,' he said, and as he looked back, he made the face of indigestion and held his hand to his stomach; five females smiled and blew kisses to say they cared. Once outside a pale light shone in their direction. 'This way Tandiette.'

Tandiette's eyes adapting to see past the light. He was tall, dressed in a flowing robe and sandals.

'Thomas,' Ashland said. 'This is my daughter, the one I spoke of.'

Tandiette surprised after all the times she was nothing but a servant girl away from Dearling City.

'Pleased to meet you,' he said. 'Follow me, the streets have ears,' and he led the way. They stopped as he opened a heavy wooden door, and they followed him in. A small room, dimly lit. 'Take a seat. Sorry I don't have refreshments, but this is not my dwelling, merely for storage purposes, or...' and he stared at Tandiette and she looked at her father.

'So, talk,' Ashland said. 'Tell me who the traitor is, the one giving away our secrets?'

'I followed your advice and set the lure of a treasure within Dearling City.'

Tandiette stared at her father and said, 'How could you father?'

He ignored her and said to Thomas, 'And?'

'Every messenger has ten of our eyes on him,' and he turned to Tandiette, 'or her. We followed to see who turns up. So far nothing. Whoever is controlling the Unworthy must be fearsome in ways we have no knowledge of, able to move from our world and theirs without raising suspicion.'

'Keep me informed. We won't stand a chance if they find a way into Dearling City.'

Tandiette stewed as they talked, before she boiled, 'All this,' and she waved her hand, 'you take for granted. This that rests on the bones of the grey moon's toil, and now…' she could hardly say the words, 'Dearling City.'

'Tandiette!'

'No Ashland, your daughter speaks the words of truth. We in the Golden City haven't always been blinded by wealth. Once, a very long time ago, we were humble, another city trying to survive. Greed is insidious, treats for the willing we said. Few here realize if we continue this way we will be swallowed by our own selfishness, consumed by an insatiable beast who sits atop the rabble outside, those fermented souls tasked with trying to survive, and we fiddle, while plague wipes out those he takes from. We are going to fall, no matter the height of our walls or the amount of provisions we have stored; and I leave you young girl with a proverb from the times of old, when dragons roamed and wrongdoers were pieces of toast for their saliva. It is said…Once in a generation, to tame the flame you must breathe the light to free the soul,' and he turned back to Ashland, 'but first we must scratch out the evil in our midst,' as Tandiette pulled her sleeves low to a shiver that ran through her bones.∞∞∞∞

Chapter 12

Baby grows up

'When the moons go to ground and the peasants won't pay, we dig the graves to another day.

Ooh rah rah, ooh rah rah.

Tear down the trees, take out their souls... break the feed to Dearling's needs.

Ooh rah rah, ooh rah rah.'

The vegetation clawed back to the constant drizzle of insect bites and the frosted eyes of an Unworthy.

Raval peered and said, 'Clear.'

'Move up and bring the weapon.'

Ten Unworthy held a piece of the workings, the size of two Dearlings. Three carried the metal bow, never bent unless by the machine. A quiver of sharp pointed heads protruded to an unseen rock as they stumbled and embedded the jagged head into a leg. 'Ah,' his piercing cry sending a crisp chill through the fat nasally rodents being dragged.

The axe rotated from ten feet. One end of the arrow's shaft ripped off as an Unworthy rolled and groaned in the dirt.

Without a word Devlin approached. 'Oaf,' he said and bent to study the injury and retrieve his weapon, his cold eyes staring down on Barden. He stood to his full height, head and shoulders above the others, and swung, the arrowhead fell, silent to an unconscious Unworthy. He bent down to pull out the valued metal head wiping the drips. 'Leave him. Let our Arogons have a feed...So this is the entrance?'

Raval ignored the metal head still dripping in his leader's hand and with a flicker of his cold eyes he said, 'Yes,' and looked back to the two hundred groaning impatient for battle. 'Single file from here on in,' and into the tunnel the mighty two hundred went. He stopped where the tunnel divided, and fifty pointy weapons were felt by the complainants and the mighty piled up in the gloom.

'Light the torches,' Devlin ordered.

Up ahead Raval felt for the scratches of the Kreton. 'This way,' and they followed, first walking, then, claws and knees as the tunnel narrowed.

'Wait. Go back,' and a hundred Unworthy were forced backwards to the grumbles of confusion. 'Let me open up this space' he said, and Devlin swung his axe hard against the tunnels wall. Perinite fired in the hell of a volcano, retaliated. His axe-head shattered, pieces ricocheting, biting the side of his face. He wiped the dribble. 'Hand me your weapon, Raval.'

'But?'

'You won't be needing it,' and he grabbed the sword, 'being the first,' and he pushed another two Unworthy between him and Raval, each giving up their weapon, to squeeze on their bellies to the dribble of light ahead. 'We'll pass them out. Go... go feed the-need.'

Raval flat, looked out... Bright swirls of light, track clear, deadly quiet and they waited. He peaked his nose and smelt. Nothing but the occasional taste of decay and an old kill. Quiet calm. He scrambled out... Low a large rat in the land of the dinosaur and more, much more.

Biscuit glided, hidden by the light, his domain, below, home twenty miles ahead. The jungle reached out in meaning, because all that breathed the air in this land, knew he had come of age. Flying creatures often went to ground at a single whiff, and when he felt the urge, he was quick and merciful.

'Set up over there,' Raval pointed. 'I saw the creature attack,' and he walked to mark the spot, 'here,' he said. 'Backs to the wall. That will give us a clear shot, and, no surprises.' Another twenty scrambled out of the hole. The heavy base of the machine churning, dirt stirred into a mushroom of activity as six Unworthy pulled on the rope.

'Bubble roots of toads, critters of goblins,' they spewed as they struggled with the fit, and without another word they pulled a shaft and cranked the device ready.

Raval aimed and pulled the trigger, an arrow shot twenty feet disappearing into the jungle. 'Don't waste the shafts,' Devlin ordered brushing himself off, emerging from the tunnel. 'One genius has to fetch that.' The group looked at each other and kicked the runt in the direction. 'Load another shaft and if he complains, you have a target.' The runt looked back snarling and turned to follow the trodden vegetation close to where it had vanished.

Twenty miles to a dragon takes but twenty seconds when the eyes of the jungle shout out in the language of their kind. Biscuit's eyes narrowed to single slits. He dove low over the tree tops, wing tips occasionally shearing a branch, near matching terrain, as he followed the complaints, his very presence silencing what an apex predator fears not, and... as he approached home... he heard the shouts of the stupid, for they did not know this land of the lost was his.

'What,' and Raval turned to the shape that blocked the light. 'Fire, fire,' he yelled. Biscuit banked and shook his head for his stomach was full; two Woolly-fouls and a Grubnut. He burped when the steel stung, caught between two scales and he faulted mid-flight to growl, to the metal piercing his side as he turned his head down to bite the arrow clean off; for an injured dragon shows no mercy. Clumsy claws of cranking creaked as they fired again, but, this time, he was ready, designed with the elegance of wisdom he caught the projectile between his teeth and bit what they thought unbreakable. Ity bits of distemper rained down. Breath painful, he flew high as they cranked another time. Biscuit sucked another breath, side on fire he smoked the mist to a cinder's crisp.

Pea from above, the fog rolled down. 'Where is it,' shouted all about. Two enraged red eyes glowed thick within the mist. Three pushed the contraption in an attempt to follow. For whatever they were the need of survival revelled within their stupidity that few could fathom. One desperate clench, pulled the trigger. Blue flame turned white hot as the metal melted to wash a rinse of sear all over a runt. Cranking creaks filtered desperate as four ran within a circle like overwound flaming candles. Biscuit landed to review the stupid ones. Out of the smog he loomed as Raval lifted his sword and Devlin pushed another three into the towering creature's path. Their weapons swung like insects being splattered by the paw of a lost Tidan. Flung to squash onto the rock walls of home. He breathed out again, a furnace where only cinders remained.

'Retreat, retreat! Out of my way,' as Devlin pulled two out of the hole and threw them to be gobbled by this demon as he shouted 'Retreat,' and scrambled in head-first. Safe he thought with the opening closing white hot behind, setting to the red of molten rock and he could smell the burn of his cowardice, with all that remained turned to slag that once held an opening. Biscuit stared back at the flames as he coughed out a toothpick of sword. Up he flew to douse his home, but unknown, below the ash one thing moved. A runt... gaining a sense, shocked, desperate, between flaming trees, only to trip, sprawling and when the sea above came crashing down, the one and only exit waited. Washed flat the runt stood, Biscuit's sharp eye saw the movement, but too late as the Unworthy scrambled, on all fours, to disappear into an exit too small for a full-grown dragon to fit. Surrounded, bathed deep inside the tunnels overlap with the light barrier he sucked in deep uncontrollable breathes. Biscuit snorted at the entrance and turned to lick his wound and returned to see what other evil creature was lurking ready to threaten his home.

The runt staggered forward, head hitting rocks, unable to see, beyond caring, far up ahead noises. Happy laughter and cries of another's kind. Searching, searching he moved forward, in the pitch black to another kind, because to go back, to go back and his body shook with the thought.

Dearling square busy, school was out. Parents and children played. A group of Dearlings opening up an eatery, ready for the evening rush. A mother bounced a baby on her knee when the first scream erupted, only to be cut dead by the silence, as a six foot four runt staggered, then, stood to his full height for a moment. Dizzy, he stumbled again, eyes burnt, claws outstretched as he stared trying to fathom. Once a humble being that succumbed, no amount of reasoning was ever going to reverse, but deep inside a tiny speck of light ignited to undo a feeling to what a very long time ago he was, a once respected Tidan.

Ten Dearlings ran to reach for their bows when the Screech-horn was blown. Arrows dipped in the poison chalice, for how else were they to bring down such a creature and without another sound the bite from ten bit into the beast from above, for a moment, he remembered, who he was before the creature took hold, and in the finality of a sigh his eyes stilled for ever more.∞∞∞∞

Chapter 13

Truth be known

Ismelda reared, alarmed. 'Shh,' Tandiette said stroking her Ductile as they dismounted. 'Father I don't know what's wrong. We timed our descent perfectly between the ash eruptions. Do you know what, I have this strange feeling,' and she stroked Ismelda again, 'Maybe it's nothing.'

'Come Tandiette we need to alert the council to be on the look-out. I'll send Parian back to feed and water Ismelda, to calm her distress.'

They walked ahead and twenty feet inside the exit. 'Who goes there?'

'What do you mean, "Who goes there?" Can't you recognize Tandiette and me,' Ashland said.

'Oh,' as two Dearlings struggled to move the heavy barricade.

'What's happened,' Ashland demanded.

'We are under Dearling Law. Any questions must be directed through the council, and all outsiders are under house confinement. That includes you two.'

'We'll see,' Ashland grumbled as he walked Tandiette to their home.

Claritine stood, hands on hips in the doorway. 'How dare they, shut my twins and me like common criminals, and they look more Dearling, than a Dearling. I mean to say?' Ashland pushed past as Claritine shuddered, not wanting to touch Tandiette. 'Keep your daughter separate,' she said. 'We all know she's possessed, and maybe by the same thing that creature was taken with.

'What creature?'

'That foul smelling, snarling thing that entered our square. Right in front of the kids,' and she shook uncontrollable.

'An Unworthy,' Parian said coming out of his room to the raised voices, 'and worse, they've blocked the passage to Biscuit.'

'Biscuit, what biscuit?' Claritine said.

'Oh just a treat for you my dear,' as Ashland's forced a smile, anything but convincing to Tandiette's face dividing frown.

The twins running between Parian and Tandiette. Claritine pulled at her hair, beyond consoling. 'Keep away from your ugly sister,' she said.

Ashland placed his hand on Tandiette's shoulder and said, 'Come daughter, it's time to set things straight. Confinement or no confinement,' and he nodded for her to follow.

They walked out... every Halfling's home guarded. 'Sorry, we have orders for all outsiders to be placed under house arrest. No exceptions.'

'No exceptions, is it Sunny Bill. You will have to strike me down before you will stop me talking to the Grand Rous.'

'He looked at his companion, grip tightened on his diminutive sword, but Tandiette blocked their path.

86

'Father knows best,' she said.

'Tandiette stop,' Ashland said. 'We have important information for him and the grand circle of leaders.'

The diminutive guard looked at his peer who saw Tandiette's eyes redden.

'Maybe we should let them reveal their news to our leader.'

'Rodon, you go. I'll stay here guarding.'

The Grand Rous quarters located inside the largest cavern in Dearling City. A quarts statue of him stared down on Tandiette as she passed, such was his influence. The female Dearling receptionist sat waiting.

Rodon spoke first, 'Ashland and his daughter request an audience with the Grand Rous.'

'He's in a meeting, not to be disturbed,' and she looked at Ashland who she'd seen on many occasions before.

'We have urgent, no imperative information that is essential in keeping us safe. I can't stress how important.'

'I'll be breaking all the rules and could lose my job,' she said.

'Better than losing your life,' Tandiette said, two scales falling to her desk when Tandiette's clenched fist rattled her inkwell.

Shocked to a lip's quiver. 'I'll see. Wait here Ashland,' her eyes elsewhere, anywhere but an irritated Tandiette. She disappeared for a moment and returned ruffled as voices beyond echoed, as if she was responsible. 'Follow me,' she said.

'No need I know the way,' and they turned the sharp corner to a corridor. Decorated weapons hung, draped by the cloaks of honour all male Dearling once wore; that was before, when things were so different to the present.

87

Ashland pushed the heavy double doors and they swung open.

The Grand Rous stood. 'Ashland you have no place at the table in this meeting.'

'Oh don't I,' and he looked at the mixture of races, all representatives, once, from Dominicon's other lands, Frogmotto, Bristletow, Gristledom and Tiltertop. They wriggled, blighted, he knew, with characteristics that would never allow them on Tidan. Escapees, deserters or envoys, he was never quite sure when the Dearlings offered them asylum.

'Our very city has been breached,' the Grand Rous said, one good tooth rumbled by the gurgling indigestion that followed.

'Yes, but by what I was told, by only one. Why only one?'

'Isn't one more than enough, and thus, we have sealed the city so no others will come.'

Ashland growled, 'They will come all right. In their hundreds, if not thousands, unless you hear what I have to say.'

'Why should we listen to you with all your so called, connections? Have you helped any of these countries,' and he swung his arm, to each and every representative.

'I am sorry for your pain,' his eyes connecting around the room, 'at the hands of the Unworthy, but we have all suffered and his eyes fell on Tandiette in that moment. She blinked trying to be strong. 'We may have a way of defeating this illness once and for all, or at very least, stopping it in its tracks...'

'Too late,' the Grand Rous interrupted, 'we have made an order to make a deal.'

'A deal,' Ashland's face screwed so even Tandiette could see herself in his expression. 'Who can make a deal with an Unworthy?'

'There is one amongst us that has contact within the leadership, and he assures us Dearling city will not be touched, and the one that broke in, a warning, nothing more. All we have to do is give up our Halflings, and some others who shall not be named, here.'

'You can't,' Tandiette's voice cracking to almost broken.

'Your daughter has no right to speak,' the Grand Rous said.

'It's all right Tandiette,' and Ashland turned back. 'Trust the word of an Unworthy, or anyone that deals with them, you must be joking,' and he looked around the table trying to find a sign, but there was none.

'We can and we will when there is no other alternative.'

Ashland looked at Tandiette as if for permission before turning with the words, 'We have a dragon.'

Confused chatter in five dialects broke out all about before, The Grand Rous said, 'How can a legend live when a thousand years of silence is all we've ever known.'

'It does and it is our salvation.'

'He, father... he.'

'And he is our salvation.'

'So you say, and who will stop us being devoured, if what you say is true. We will take our chances with the Unworthy,' the Grand Rous voice croaked louder accompanied by one bloodshot eye quivering, about to pop.

Tandiette's leap, unreasonable, irrational, desperate, a teenager of another kind. The circular table her floor as she looked down on the Grand Rous, eyes alight to every wrong in her life. In front, an overwhelming need to be exorcised, and as he opened his mouth to speak her claws pushed through the toe of her shoes and bit into the heavy wooden table. Words coughed into nothing but smoke as the Grand Rous choked on her hot breath, eyes bulging to a one good tooth nearly lost. With her voice found, she said, 'I will.'

'Tandiette come down…' she heard the voice she'd learnt every lesson from, with the thing she was, resolving, and she looked to his face and stepped between two shaking delegates

'Guards, guards!' The Grand Rous yelled as Tandiette looked into her father's eyes.   'We have done our best, my daughter. There is no protecting those that lay with the enemy.'   'Guards.'   Four Dearlings, armed with swords drawn entered. 'Bind their hands and escort them back to their home… and reinforce the guards there by two,' and he looked at Tandiette again whose claws had fully retracted. 'No six.'∞∞∞

Chapter14

Escape

'What happened?' Claritine pacing, six Dearling guards outside fiddling with chains and locks.

'Untie these, Parian,' Ashland said.

'The meeting went badly?' Claritine glaring though the window.

'Tandiettes as well Parian?'

'No need little brother,' as she handed him two broken ties covered in scales. With two fingers he carefully placed them in the trash.

'We have found out their plans and it's not pretty.'

'Who's not pretty?' Claritine said.

'Us, all of us, the twins included,' Ashland said. 'We are the offerings to the Unworthy, so the pure bloods can be saved.

'Me and my twins, never… Oh god,' and she thought for a moment. 'I'll go, I will, they must see, they must. We are not all alike…' and she looked at Tandiette. 'They must.'

She rattled the front door as two Dearlings yelled, 'Stop.'

'I demand to speak to the Grand Rous myself.'

'Ha, ha, ha,' and one guards sharpened sword poked through the door. 'Move back Tidan, or next time will be your last.' A pin prick of bloodstain soaked to spread through her dress.

'Let me help,' Tandiette said.

'No, I don't need your help. Keep your hands to yourself, this is all your fault,' and she tore a shred of garment and wrapped it around her leg. The twins ran to their injured mother's side, crying. 'So, this is how we end husband? Locked underground to be roasted for dinner by an Unworthy,' and the twins sobs grew, inconsolable.

'No time to dally Claritine. We need to leave,' Ashland said.

'Leave how can we leave?' She said.

'Parian show her,' and he snuffed the candle. The never to be doused candle, every Dearling dwelling kept lit. The smoke column twisted, another lost idol to the sacred fire altar of the Dearling gods. Without the trickle of heat, a working's of a master craft-man's hand, couldn't hold the balance of the counterweight, and like magic the slither of a black passage opened.

'A secret passage. How do you think father and Tandiette could disappear, by magic?'

'What else aren't you telling me?'

'Claritine grab the twins, there is no other way.' Ashland said as she saw Tandiette being engulfed by the black, then Parian.

'Come Roselyn and Riesel, follow your half-brother,' with every line of worry wanting to blame, but when she turned. 'I know when you look at Tandiette your eyes say much more than when you look at the twins, but worse, me.'

'Go,' Ashland said, and he pushed her into the dark, 'Another time, Claritine. Not here,' and his hand released the latch. The rock wall fell shut with the taste of dust behind and the black of future ahead. Never to be opened to them again, he thought.

'Oh... that horrid smell? Cover your mouths children,' Claritine said, her face alight with the opening's glow.

Nasally snorts of tossed larva, hot with a volcano's breath. 'Stay close to the wall,' Parian said as they crabbed their way.

Ahead Tandiette disappeared into the black of another tunnel and they followed, Ashland at the rear. She stopped twenty feet in. 'I can smell them ahead,' she said. 'Three Dearling guards.'

'You do? All I smell is the rotten eggs of the volcano,' and Parian held onto the twins in the dark before Claritine, feeling her way, walked into all three. 'Stop,' he whispered.

Tandiette squinted, as she spoke like a fairy into Parian's ear. 'They've barricaded the tunnel to Biscuit. I just hope they haven't sealed it for good.'

'Eight pounds of feed to produce one pound of meat. Never. Cut off the hand that feeds Dearling City, they wouldn't last a week,' Parian whispered back.

'I'll take care of them,' Ashland taking the lead.

'No father, one scratch from those arrows...' and she didn't dare think. 'I'm quicker,' and she ran.

'Did you hear that?' All three Dearling ears turning to listen. The growl louder this time causing two rocks to fall as they hurried to pull three bows tight, poison freshly dipped, dripping from the arrow tip. Ready to shoot, whatever made that sound beyond the barricade.

Out of the dark she came, before one of them had a chance to blink, she slid, taking all three Dearlings down and as they fell, arrows shot; weapons without targets, sprayed, porcupine quills to a Halfling's skill and when a sword was drawn she let one fist knock a snap of sleep into each and every chin. "No blood spilt here," she thought.

Ashland came running. 'No need, father. All is taken care of.'

Parian saw... 'Your leg,' and like her last breath, the sharp pain spread.

'The arrow heads deep Tandiette,' Ashland said.

'And the poison, poor love, she'll die, like an Unworthy won't she?' Claritine said emerging.

Tandiette felt the lethal salty spit of the Venom bush rise in her legs, mouth and arms until her brain was filled by the taste.

'Lethal to anyone but a Dearling,' Ashland said... 'Or a Halfling,' and he smiled. The taste will linger though,' and with that thought he pulled on the shaft, Tandiette flinching as the arrow head came clean out.

'Parian your shirt,' and he wrapped the wound.

'Father careful, the poison,' Tandiette said in a whimper.

He stroked her hair and touched her ears. 'You are your father's daughter, I have nothing to fear,' and Claritine went cold with his expression.

'And, who are these, the forgotten deserts,' and she hugged the twins. Stay close to me my babies,' she said.

'How is your leg Tandiette. Do you think you can walk?'

She tested her weight. A sharp pain pressed back. 'Maybe,' she said.

'Parian help me push these logs clogging the passage.' Together, they huffed and puffed with all their effort, but the logs sat stubborn. 'If we can't shift these,' and Ashland's desperate voice was all Tandiette heard as she bit her lip and three pushed as one, until, the one holding her breath was overwhelmed, and she let out a scream so shrill all around thought the ceiling would surely fall.

Beyond a growl reverberated, air broken by the force, and for a moment she forgot her pain. 'Biscuit,' she cried, standing in a gaping hole where once there was none.

'Your leg,' Ashland said, and he leant down to tie off her leaking bandage.

'Never mind her leg. What was that horrid sound beyond?' Claritine said gripping the twins so tight their faces ballooned to a pinkish-red.

'You are about to be schooled Claritine,' Parian said.

'Schooled? What school?'

'The school of beasts only a mother could love. Right Tandiette?'

'I'm not really a mother,' and she thought, 'more a conduit.'

'Conduit? What the heck?' Parian said.

'I read it in one of father's books. "Whatever it said," that word, that's what I am.'

'Whatever,' as Parian pushed Claritine and the twins towards the Light barrier ahead, shimmering. The true meaning of a baby hidden, awash in the vail of confused ripples.

'Stop! Don't take another step,' Ashland yelled running up to Claritine. 'This is for our children's sake,' and he looked deep into Claritine's eyes with a feeling she thought she'd lost. 'No one really knows why,' he said, 'but the laws of our grandfathers have really sound reasons behind them.' He kneeled in front of the twins. 'We all have to hold our breath, not for long, just while we pass through this curtain of light,' and his hand dissolved into the swirl of sticky bright discolouration. 'Do you think you can take a really deep breath and hold it for ten seconds?'

'Sure father, if you say so,' and they both looked to Claritine for reassurance.

'You too, Claritine.'

A blank look followed as she said, 'Follow your father's instructions children.'

'Tandiette, Parian, you go ahead, we never know, just in case.'

'Schools in,' Parian said.

'Now children. If I count to five can you hold your breath? One, two, three, four and five…' and they sucked in a big breath. 'Excellent. Now this time for real,' and as he counted, they linked hands. One by one, they disappeared, swallowed by the light…

The scream pierced, then went dead. Biscuit stared down. Two twin's cheeks, overfilled, cowering beside the still body of their mother.

'Breathe twins, breath,' Ashland said.

Biscuit bent down and sucked the scent of each as Claritines eyes opened. The sliding slits of Biscuits pupils stared directly into hers, eye to eye, and abruptly she resumed her former state… Unconscious.

'No Biscuit, these are not others. No eating!'

He croaked, 'I can smell the blood of your father running in the little ones. The other… looks tasty.'

'That's their mother, Claritine. No Biscuit,' and Tandiette frowned.

He snorted and limped away.

'You're hurt?' Tandiette said.

'And you?' Biscuit replied.

Biscuit turned and lay down beside her. Softly he lowered his face, tongue reaching to rip at her bandage and lick her dried blood clean. Tender she flinched, instinctive, to nestle into his side as her tongue stretched out to taste his near healed scar. 'How,' she asked.

'No need to fret, mother. I have bitten off the claw of the devils.' He lifted his head and stood to his full height, and with one wing stretched, he pointed∞∞∞∞

.

The Last Dragon's egg

Chapter 15

Time waits for no one

'Roasted roaches,' Raval looked up to the swirly specs filling the sky. 'Raise the alarm,' he growled.

Arogons with riders barely seen. Sleepy Unworthy pulled at their pants and yawned to the growing numbers, like insects in the wind. Higher still, winged creatures strained at reins. Violent flaps to vortex swirls. Currents between the worlds. Fires kept alive, fanning the hot air balloons of airships. Deep in the bowels, slaves, handcuffed.

Melinda forced two fingers between the weave. 'I can't see a damn thing.'

Seraphina replied, 'I think I know. We are going to my daughter's home world. I can feel it in my bones.'

'And what does the cripple boy think?' Melinda said.

'I have a name. Radian,' and he wrestled his body, healed broken. 'I can still move faster than you Melinda.'

A tired smile crossed her face. 'So you can... I wonder why they have been feeding us up,' and she shuddered to think.

'Bring them down. Over there,' Devlin pointed. 'They can start work on clearing the forest. Take this water for the palm oil seedlings,' as he looked to the sky again, because someone else was on his way.

Whips cracked as the slaves were unloaded, "What a waste," the beady eye of an Unworthy narrowed with a thought, as he snorted, 'They are fatter,' and dribbled, urge so strong, almost willing to have his head ripped off by his leader, but with the wisdom of a crocodile he snapped at the three slaves with the word, 'Move.'

'Did you see how he looked at us,' Melinda whispered.

'Ignore him,' Seraphina said. 'Keep up Radian,' and he crabbed his way, legs the shape of a cockroach.

Swirling high above... 'Sweep the area my pretty, I want to see for myself... and check that caves entrance one more time.'

Like a dot they appeared above the encampment... growing...

'Take a look,' Radian said. 'That's the creature. The big boss. I saw him give out orders,' and they stared across the freshly cleared field.

His Arogon landed with the Lordling swirling his cane. The whole encampment stopped as Devlin bent to one knee before his master.

'Up stupid.' Sir Erin all but a disguise for the weak of mind, not here, he knew. 'How goes the fields, we have orders to fill?'

'They will be another month before ready,' Devlin growled as his master scanned the encampment, with the newly transferred slaves a point of interest, and he raised his cane and pointed.

'Those three. Keep them separate, I have plans for them.'

'Yes master,' and with the grumble of commands two of the ugliest Unworthy Melinda had ever seen marched over to take them away. Radian thought about fleeing; before, he would had stood a chance, now, he looked down at his crippled legs and shuffled. An obedient cockroach in the land of giant ghouls where one foot was only needed to squish him flat... and as he scurried he heard the filth busy with their business.

'So you disobeyed me, Devlin.'

'Disobeyed? No master, never.' Mesmerized he stood, the crystal of the cane drawing him in by the charm of its owners will.

'You were not to attack Dearling City, or the creature in the cave. Were you not?'

He scratched the forest of growth protruding from his face. 'The others were becoming restless. No, angry. Revenge runs in our veins like acid. We were so close to Dearling City we could all taste their blood. The mob would have ruled, and all your plans would have been lost.'

His master cast an eye on the already flourishing fields of palm oil. The Golden City would pay a pretty penny for their oil, he thought. 'So be it,' and raised his cane above his head. 'Hear Ye. Hear Ye. Hear Ye.' A voice only the ruler of the Unworthy could muster and with his cane lowered Devlin saw his future reflected in the jewel. Then with the twinkle of a mind the crystal responded, a shaft of blue so pure the clouds illuminated, startling Unworthy and prisoner alike, with all about clear to see... a forgotten god had arisen. 'We have another way of taking Dearling City,' he said, and held aloft the smouldering ear of their commander, cut clean by his surgery. Devlin had felt nothing, except his hearing was better for all the wax that poured out, and his master's greed of him. One ear, or less.

∞∞∞

'Don't touch it. It's disgusting. How could you lead my twins, your children here? Yuk.' Claritine flung the scrap of meat back to the entrance.

'This is only temporary. We will find a safer place, I promise,' Ashland said.

'And the way that beast stares.' And she held her children. 'I feel like he wants to eat me.'

'No he's completely protective of us,' Tandiette said.

'Why don't you ask him?' Parian said with a smile.

'Shut up, little brother.'

'Tandiette,' as her father's head flicked towards the entrance.

Outside Biscuit was licking his wound. 'How was the kill, tasty?' he growled.

'Yes beautiful,' Tandiette said. 'You spoil us.'

'They must have another way out, the full bloods,' Parian said emerging, careful to keep his sister between him and her dragon. 'Other than you know, the volcano,' and he stared directly into the melted rock that was once the outlet to the world above.

'Probably twenty, but they were never going to show us,' Ashland said.

'They'll be coming for us won't they?' Parian said.

'Let them come. One sign of Biscuit and they'll run right back. The pure bloods, the pure Dearling scum. We, our Halfling brothers and sisters are helpless. We have to go back,' and Tandiette kicked at the rock set like concrete.

'To go back, they would expect that. Even the way we came,' her father said.

Biscuit spread his wings and with one flap he soared, eyes searching, to the thickest part of the jungle. What's he up to she thought and with an answer he returned.

'I melt, while you open. With this,' and he threw down the tree's trunk. 'Sure, you might burn to cinders. Such is the price to open the wound to the devils lair above,' he growled, and he licked his wound one more time.

Biscuit opened his mouth while Ashland, Tandiette and Parian stood ready with the log.

'Lift,' Ashland said.

'God this twig is heavy. Are you sure you're lifting sis?'

'I'm lifting, are you,' as Biscuit breathed out the fire of the gods with a roar as the rock glowed red, then white, then molten.

'Now,' Ashland said and together they pushed the log into the molten slag. It spluttered screaming with sap spitting complaints in all directions and Ashland, the lead, feeling the heat so wild, no matter how he resisted he was toasted, well done. He slumped, useless.

'Stop,' Tandiette yelled. 'Father are you all right?' Her face glowing, eyes, slits of concern. He rolled over and she saw the blisters grow like tightening eruptions under his skin. 'Oh no. Get the water Parian?' And as he ran, 'Don't worry father we'll take care of you.'

His smile hidden in the grimace of pain, 'I know you will,' as Parian's douse was thrown like he was an out of control bush fire. He spluttered with water for words and he attempted to stand. She steadied him as they all stared at the log poking out, cooling to a charred black stick of disobedience now stuck as one with the wall.

'Useless. What were we thinking,' Tandiette's voice trailing to distraut.

'I know a way, 'Biscuit growled, 'but first you must be ready to…' and he looked to the heavens. 'Climb aboard,' he said.

She looked to her father. 'Go Tandiette. I'll be alright,' his shirt burnt to blisters dripping wet…

Between his wings she felt his heart, strong, young. 'I have a memory for everything in the past,' he growled, 'and you Tandiette, have none. An open mind, a problem solver. This Biscuit you call me can only know the mistakes made by history, not the problems of the future,' and he flapped higher. 'Tandiette your skin is a shell, let the light set you free. Free to be what you really are, a thing of nature, not one thing or another, but of three worlds with all the mistakes and beauty they hold.' They levelled out to skim below the light barrier and he turned his head so one eye could stare at her. 'You know what you must do,' and again they rose, all her reasons not to, evaporated. She sucked the light with every breath until the deepest of her cells knew the reason, to fight, to be. With her twentieth, Biscuit descended. 'It is for you to figure out who you are and what you want,' he growled.

She climbed down to see the stunned faces of her brother and father and said. 'I have been many creatures this last year, a Halfling, a Tidan, a mother, a daughter, but most of all I haven't been me and here I am, in front of you, as me as I can be.'

'Well you should keep your mouth closed because that forked tongue isn't all that becoming,' Parian said.

'Stand back little brother,' and with one wave Tandiette turned to Biscuit and said, 'Go.' He breathed out, a blowtorch to her touch and before he had reached his crescendo, she removed the pole, redirecting the tip to pierce the hole once again. A furnace worker with a black-magic wand. Every piece of fire reflected in the scales covering her body. A suit of another type. 'There. That's what I call an entrance,' and she felt for the first time her scales cool with the nodules growing on her back, an itch almost irresistible, as she looked to her full-grown baby.

'I know just how you feel,' he growled.

With two blinks of her eyes her glow returned to a shade only a mother could love. Her father closed his mouth and hid his stare, 'This... this is a two-way entrance, you know?'

'You're in no fit shape to do what needs to be done, father. Parian and I will go.'

'So much like your mother, well except for...'

'What about me,' Biscuit growled.

'I need you to stay. To protect them from whatever comes out of this opening.'

'I just hope it's us,' Parian said, testing the rock, 'Ouch. Hot. We should wait?'

'For you maybe,' and Tandiette stepped through. 'Come on don't be a wimp, daylight is burning,' and she smiled at him, then Biscuit. 'Take care of what is left of my precious family. Won't you.'

'Your wish is my command,' he growled back.

∞∞∞∞

Caged, three prisoners looked out to the tears drying on the little ones. Each child forced to stop and look on them. The reason, none had a clue. The older Halflings were next... Two hideous creatures stood watching, one held an odd shaped cane, imbedded in its head, a crystal. More filed past until there was none left, only a rotund Dearling that wore the crown of the Grand Rouse.

'There, we have given you all the Halflings?'

Devlin looked at his master, and the three caged prisoners. 'She is not here, is she,' and he rattled the cage.

The Lordling's robe swirled out as he turned on the Grand Rous. 'Rous me this rodent. You promised me she would be one of them. Didn't you,' and he thumped his cane into the ground as the gem turned to a glowing crystal. 'Filthy little critter. Off with his head.'

Devlin gripped the axe.

'No wait,' the Grand Rous squealed. 'I know where she is…' as Devlin's grip on the handle tightened to the stench of his breath, 'and…and Sir Ashland, and the family.'

The Lordling stumbled for a moment, saved by his cane. His face flickering like a screen of uncertainty, waiting, for the evil within to rise again.

He walked to the cage and stared into Seraphina's eyes, and said. 'You could have had it all, once upon a time, if you hadn't chosen him. The stupidly wonderful Sir Ashland.' Her eyes of horror stared back. 'So be it.' He turned back to face his annoyance. 'Where is Ashland and the girl, rodent? Remember, one wrong word,' and he looked at Devlin waiting for the order.

'They are in the great below. The land between heaven and hell. Where the wild beasts roam,' and he shuddered. 'Ductiles ten a penny, so beware.'

'Ductiles, ha, ha, ha. We have no fear of Ductiles,' and with a nod Devlin slapped the Grand Rous's face toward a field of twenty. Each tied to a stake waiting for their feed of Halfling leftovers.

The Grand Rous shook his head and said. 'There is talk of a creature so vicious no one dare look up when his shadow looms large, even the most ferocious beasts hide from his glare.'

'Show me this place. This great below,' The Lordling said.

'Master I will go, and take my best twenty Unworthy?'

'No Devlin. I need you here. I don't trust the others not to feed. All must stay alive… for now,' and he reached out and felt his remaining ear. Lest we forget my orders,' and he slapped at the critters feasting in Devlin's beard.

'Yes master, all must stay alive, even this rodent,' and he threw his axe as the Grand Rous jerked violently backwards with his crown falling on the ground. The axe buried itself into the last standing tree. Three squirrels scampered down and ran for the only close cover, the freshly planted palm oil shrubs.

'I will go with his majesty here,' the Lordling said, and picked up the crown to push it on his captive's head until the tears of the Grand Rous were ready to accept any plight. They walked together past the lines of shackled Halflings and into the no longer secret passage. 'Remember Rous, if one drop of that poison you Dearlings are famous for, should touch my body, then, you will have no protection from what will come. Understood?'

'Yes, no protection.'

∞∞∞∞

'I don't remember this tunnel being so long,' Tandiette said.

'Just keep your nose to the wind, being…' with a smile, 'special,' Parian said.

'Oh, shut up. There is no wind in here,' and her back itched ready to erupt with any annoyance.

They stopped. 'The entrance,' Parian said. 'Be ready to run if we see an Unworthy.'

'Run,' and Tandiette's blood boiled to embrace the opportunity, then she remembered why she couldn't, her mother. So distant, plight unknown and she refused to accept anything but, "she was alive." Every turn tainted with abject failure, piling up like the anger inside of her. "What was it her mother would do?" with the twirl of her fingers in her hair she remembered. The soft of her touch, the warmth of her body, the taste of love, and she calmed the need within.

Parian whispered, 'They're cleared away the bush. We can see clear across too... Oh no, the ones close to us. Look Glen and Georgia, shackled like Dredgeling dogs.'

'I see,' and she scanned the Unworthy fires as far as the eye could see, with a gulp, her throat caught. 'In the cage,' she gasped. 'In the cage Parian. The cage, do you see?'

'Who's in the cage?'

'Mother,' and she squinted. 'Mother and... Oh he's injured. Just look at poor Radian.'

'How can I see who's in the cage,' and he squinted too far off for any normal Halfling.

'That must be their leader. That big one, just look how the others cower in his presence. We take him out and...'

'Take him out. Look at the size of him. We wouldn't get within a blue-berry's throw of him. That's suicide Tandiette. Put a brain back in that head of yours, we have to go back and inform our father. He will know.'

She shook her head like she was shaking off a venomous tick infecting every thought. 'Your right, I know your right,' and they turned, careful not to step outside of their dark cave's shadow.

The dim couldn't hide what a Halfling brother saw. 'Are you alright Tandiette?'

She shook her head again and said, 'Yes I am. I'm sure I am,' and they walked on… past the divide and into the narrowing passage, until even for them, a squeeze. 'Ouch,' she said. 'You are treading on me.'

'Treading on your what?' and for a moment he reached out to touch and shuddered, 'Is that you?'

She thought for a second and said, 'Yes I think it is, but don't you say a word. Not a word.'

Emerging, Ashland and Biscuit were waiting, and if she thought a dragon's face could smile then that was Biscuits.

'Oh my,' Ashland said.

'Not a word, Dad,' for she had yet to see her reflection.

'Huh hmm, so how was it. Outside?' Ashland said.

'They have marched all of our fellow folk out. The Halflings,' and he looked at Tandiette in the full half-light as she stroked her dragon. 'They have them shackled like Dredgling dogs.'

'There was a big one, the boss cog. We take him out and the others will crack like the weaklings they are,' Tandiette said, nearly knocking Parian over as she turned.

'Careful,' he said.

Their voices carrying to within the cave. The twins' ears pricked and before a mother could grasp, the two Younglings ran. Five strides later, they were smacked with the face of confusion when there appeared to be another choice, one they instinctively knew was kin of a different variety.

'Eek!' cut the air. Everyone turned to see what, but the reason was stupefied to silence. They stared as she regained her voice, 'Keep your hands off my children you ugly creature.'

'It's me, Tandiette. I will never harm the twins Claritine,' her words washed like lemon juice onto Claritine's face.

'I knew you weren't right. A freak, an abomination. Children come,' and she stared again at Tandiette, with the eyes of another abomination, ten times her size, glaring down.

Biscuit growled, 'Mother it is time.'

'Time?'

'Climb up,' and she stepped, scale on scale, to blend like they matched, the big and the small... and she thought... "Not to avoid the hurtful words, but because together, we are the only choice left for my mother, Radium and a childhood of Halfling memories about to be eaten."

Biscuit flapped his wings, and as they rose, he growled, 'Beautiful creatures never know who to trust. Better they call you ugly.' Her tears slid scale to scale, down, down, spreading to dry on the wind of unfulfilled wishes... Beyond, however, on the far side, the king of the Dearlings crouched, hiding with his new master... watching.

The Lordling's crystal flickered in the blue of uncertainty. Frustrated by this world of the great below, where size matters and doubts grow, in the presence of a full grown dragon, he hid, like all the other creatures. Then, staring across the expanse, he saw a different path. One where he could have it all. ∞∞∞∞

Time waits for no one

The Last Dragon's egg

Chapter 16

The reckoning

'Look down mother, what do you see?'

'The vegetation. Creatures great and small, scurrying, hiding,' Tandiette said.

'Soon the wild ones will bow before you. Already they can sense your presence.'

She couldn't tell if she was dreaming or Biscuit was her conduit to the wild ones. She leaned in close, as one with his strong beating heart.

'A dream is a window into the mind,' he growled as if every thought she had, was his.

'Why will they bow before me,' she asked, tree tops all but a blur below, and when touched for a moment, she thought she saw.

'You mother have only just begun to open up to what will come,' and he curled his wing tips up. Sweeping higher they went to match the curve of the rock. Her fingers digging deep, clinging. Up, up they flew, until all that stood between them and the sky was an ocean contained by the translucent glare they knew as the light barrier. 'Breathe mother, breath deep,' her dragon embracing the soul of its nature. 'Big breath,' he growled to a shaft of light shining from above, and they slipped through to the chills of the deep above. Eardrums near bursting they swam up. A mother and son not sure of their origins. One, not like the other.

∞∞∞∞

Devlin turned the picture the Lordling had given him… Upside down, left to right. 'No, no,' he yelled to a mix of slaves and Unworthy, working the heavy rock. 'More steps, more steps. He needs to be seen above all. For he is our ruler.' and with a wave of a hand ten Unworthy dropped their whips and joined to work on the project. Slaves proving to be too weak, unable to shift the heavy pieces.

'Out of our way,' an Unworthy shouted, pushing at slaves. Unwanted sent sprawling, to fall into the pit of rubble making up the base.

'Oh, I can't watch,' Melinda sobbed as her friend's cries were closed over by the next boulder.

'Sacrifice empowers a throne with a sense of importance,' Devlin said and walked the first five steps to stand atop the cries succumbing and he turned the drawing one more time, satisfied.

'Monster,' Melinda said, her hollow cheeks yet to be filled by the extra rations.

Seraphina sat silent as she spat on her hand and with the other lifted the shackle to allow the moisture to reach the broken skin. Irritant quelled, she said softly, 'On this world there are things about that are far deadlier than that creature. A mother knows when a child is close.'

'A child?'

'It's a long story.'

From the bottom of the cage. 'You mean Tandiette, don't you?'

∞∞∞∞

Biscuit's head broke the surface, close by the shore. Tandiette spluttered as she clung and sucked two breathes. Her dragon waded out shaking his head, body and tail, Tandiette's grip torn, flung, rag-dolling twenty feet before he blinked. 'Oh sorry,' he quietly growled, his heavy steps sunk by the soft sand, saliva wetting her body in a lick of sandpapered tenderness.

She wiped what he had missed, and said, 'I don't know this place, Biscuit. We need to find our bearings,' and as she said, she felt her back erupt like it was trying to answer her. As much as she tried, she couldn't reach the annoyances firing out of each shoulder blade. With one hand she pushed her elbow to scratch...

'Your wings aren't ready,' he growled.

'Wings?' for the first time, caught on a ripple, a reflection... she stared for a moment at the floating distortion. 'Oh my god... I am that thing, Claritine said I was. She was right,' her voice trailing to an oceans lap. 'I'll never be royal, no queen, no crown, no destiny, a beast so trapped I can't see past my last misdeed. I don't belong, a Halfling so queer, feet so strange I'm bogged in my own fear.'

He bent to sooth her growing nodules with his tongue and growled low. 'There was an ancient proverb. Better to be ugly in beautiful times than beautiful in ugly times. It is for you to decide what times we live in and how beautiful you want to be. Here, climb up mother, let me be your wings.'

They rose on an eddy, an ocean to one side, a cradle mountain the other. Twirling smoke blossomed wanting to finger her needs. 'That way Biscuit, follow the ash.' His wings trimmed and pitched toward the cloud, her anticipation spreading within his every sense. 'We take out the big one first and the others will fall like dominoes.' Clouds freshening to the taste of grit smoked determination with only one outcome. Hers.

Off in the distance the Halfling's ears pricked. Eyes strained, and in a realisation, squealed. A hazy Unworthy awoke from an infected stupor, screams filling his ears with shackled Halflings running for cover, only to be cut down by their leg-irons. He ran for the Windglass horn and blew. A deep hollow resonance poured out to stone deafening indifference as one Unworthy turned to see. For a moment the horn was silent as the guard growled loud, 'The beast, the flying beast from the cave...'

'Stay low Biscuit, we've been spotted...' and as she looked... 'Confidence has betrayed them, their arrows and quivers are out of reach.' Biscuit swooped lower, her every command was his, near touching their foe's futile wave of sword and axe, for she needed to see more. The Halflings screams drowning with the harmonized drone from another breath on the Windglass when she first saw, her mother. Caged like some poor animal. She strained, closer. Her mother not screaming like the others, but smiling... Tandiette for a second confused, as she thought, her mother knows the truth of who she really is. Satisfied she turned her attention elsewhere... 'There the big one, he's the one Biscuit. Take him out and victory will be ours.'

Biscuits wings stroked the air one more time and they banked for attack, but in that moment, she felt her mother's voice shout above the terror,' No Tandiette. No!'

'Stop Biscuit there must be something else. Somebody else,' she hesitated. 'Destroy their bows and arrows first. Then, she saw, desperate captives in a chain gang, licked by the whips of brutes, and a frosty chill ran down her

116

backbone to the very end of her tail. 'Father,' she cried. Down to her right exiting the cave, her father, Parian, Claritine and the twins, pushed by a grotesque Unworthy and she could feel the evil emanating like the decay of death.

The Lordling's eyes narrowed and looked to the heavens, she felt its glare turn to them. Biscuits crisp flight stuttered, for he knew, and in that moment, he banked away, for their very lives depended on every move he made, because Tandiette didn't know, who she was.

'Why Biscuit,' Tandiette gasped.

The Lordling swirled and held aloft his cane to the sky, the blue jewel glowed, Unworthy far and wide dived for cover. Biscuit felt the bite, Tandiette and dragon sideways, she dangled, fingers clinging to Biscuit, as he completed a "three hundred and sixty degree," rotation. Right side up once more, she saw, 'Oh Biscuit your wing, the hole…' and with every breath he swallowed they dropped twenty feet. She looked back to her father and mother disappearing in the distance, the burning blue pulse broke the air once more.

'Ahh' Biscuit groaned. The jungle below loomed as his eyes rolled back and they dropped through the canopy, dark branches lashing their bodies and her thoughts ran to his as she avoided a line of tree trunks. Crashing, the lush ground cover parted. Wild mulberries filled her face and she looked up. Leaves like rain, to settle, quiet. Not a sound. She lay still with all about twirling in her head, when, out of an arm's reach, a stabbing sound of a baby's moan.

'Biscuit, my beautiful Biscuit, what have they done,' and she cupped both hands trying to return his life's energy pouring all over her. She grabbed a handful of leaves and shoved them into the gaping hole.

He opened his eyes, every move a groan as he raised on the fold of a good wing and tried to lick her face, but even his tongue wouldn't reach. The more she packed with leaves the more he lost, until all she had left to fill the wound was her tears.

'Don't cry mother, it is my time,' he growled.

'No, no, no, don't say that.'

'I have a gift for you. You are ready,' and he gasped. 'Power comes not from the breath of fire, being big, strong, or flying free,' he gasped again, 'but the desire to gift a brain so beautiful as yours, with a reason to fulfil our history and use the wisdom wisely.' Shaking, every word tailing to a groaning whisper, and he breathed in one more time. 'Nature is timeless, not stupid,' and he gulped. 'She has a price to be paid, to undo all that has been done; and that price is you, my beautiful little mother. One of three worlds,' and he lifted his head one final time. 'My gift comes with a warning,' and he blinked with eyes so big she could see her reflection. 'Happiness is the quiet between the thoughts,' and his lids fell heavy.

'No, no, Biscuit,' her tears his. 'You are my life, my only friend, my baby,' and she caressed his chest with every breath shallower. She stretched out, trying to will, another, like it was hers... Stilled moments died in the silence... Sounds... her own sobs. She lay confused as they dried when a distant reason raised an ugly reminder... The Windglass called out... Her mind so numb it had clogged. Clogged by something ancient. She fell, trying to resurrect a thought. Images flooded, every deed a dragon needed to survive filling her head and she thought. I can do this...No... I need to do this. She picked herself up and began to run, breathing fire to anything standing in her path as the blistering emotion exploded into the eruption of two misshapen back nodules. Bursting forth her wings, a butterfly on her first day, vegetation no longer a barrier. She rose to view the cleared fields, budding palm oil plants blossoming like weeds, and a Lordling barking orders.

Ten Arogons had found their riders. Unworthy, armed with bows no Halfling could bend, arrows the size of her, each with a steel fired head. Her wings so fresh they dried in flight, and without an ounce of practise. Somewhere deep within, Biscuit's words broke, "A gift." The touch of ten thousand years of Dragon-Dom now dwelled in one. She flexed her tips, grace so small even a Lordling dismissed her as a bird, but not an Arogon's eye trained on a rider's command. The first squawked, alerting the others to her presence.

Ten verses one, not very fair, but do I care, she thought, looking back to where her baby lay lifeless. 'For you my precious.'

The largest approached first, rider stretching on a bow and firing. Tandiette's reaction instinctive as she paused mid-flight to allow the arrow to pass, harmless. Unworthy snarled with crooked feet digging into the soft underbelly of their Arogons. The bird's sharp claws reached out with a rider's guiding reign. 'Take this,' Tandiette whispered under a breath and expelled a pure flame. Startled, the poorly trained wild creature reared, terrified. The rider cast off, plummeting to the palm oil "splat" of plants below. With the wisdom of a dragon filling her head she let forth a paralysing scream of a maturing dragon, 'AAaiiee.' I am not afraid, she told herself, and, the Unworthy who thought they were the masters of their

Arogons, were wrong. Each and every bird reacted the same, casting the rider to earth, for someone else controlled their minds. Someone, so ancient, they hadn't known in their lives before.

The lordling squinted, found out he shouted, 'Shoot,' and two hundred arrows filled the sky. She looked up to the raindrops from hell, breath hot, vaporising the shafts for twenty feet, enough for her to fit unscathed on the path to her parents. Ten seconds at most, she thought, before the next round were reloaded. Too late for him, the ugly one, shouting orders. His weapon hidden, for she did not see, nor the blue gem atop of the cane, also ancient. She flapped her wings, a thousand yards out, to the sear of his eyes glare. Held aloft, by a claw, the staff of a demi-god revealed as he unleashed the power of the stone. A moth in the headlight, caught, helpless for a second, she flapped. The power filled every cell of her body, except one wing, for unique matters when she was the minnow of his target. Squirming she wriggled free of the blue monster's glow. Desperate, precious senses shortened by the tick of time as the rain of a hundred missiles fell, metal tips sharpened to kill. Half a breath was all she had left in her flame. The sting of an arrow to a free wing bit, and like all wounded moths she went to ground. Ten, nine, she counted down a hundred yards off her prey, but on the run, she knew... too late... Lost, desperate she yelled in a dragon's breath of an octave above her baby's.

'Let my parents go!'

The creature most hideous wrapped a claw around his staff and laughed, pointing his weapon directly at her. 'Who be your parents?'

'Don't tell him,' her mother yelled.

'So, there you are, child all grown up,' and he laughed, 'Ha, ha, ha. Say your farewells little dragon girl,' and with his weapon full frontal, the blue flame exploded.

All she felt was the force boring into her chest, taking her breath, raising her up. Every cell invaded, fired by the power, her will wanting to explode, with a mother's cry of, 'No!'

Her body racked, arms and wings stretched to breaking, the blue force beyond containment as she smelt the blue flames burn out through the ends of her fingertips. All those on the ground looked up to see her stretched into a blue star streaming dragon crystal like confetti onto the naked ground below. Her father reached into Seraphina's cage and held her mother's hand and said, 'Don't watch my love. Turn your head away.'

She just smiled back and said. 'My grandparents were right, my handsome prince, I am a believer.'

Tandiette's head flung back, four hundred feet in the air, blue sky filling her eyes, the searing sparks shooting out like black cloud's thunder, and she moved a finger. The Lordling's crystal fluttered as his claw tightened, trying to crush every last drop, it blinked at him and refused, near useless.

His face drooped as if his world had ended, when he turned and said, 'Fire.'

A thousand bows released... stilted a little dragon awaited her fate... as she felt every one of the arrows, only to ask... 'Why am I not hurt?' Torn wing whole again and she stared at her arms and body, all arrows bent and busted on the ground below.

'Without a scratch?' her mother whispered in the knowing her daughter was the embodiment of every dragon that ever lived. One of three worlds, where legends live, and she was about to show what a legend felt.

Tandiette shone, a diamond in the sky. Wings intact she spread to descend. Ahead her nemesis, her family, but behind… she couldn't dare think the thought… and again she looked at the reason why.

The Lordling was shaking his cane, a crystal dull, dead, for the power of the changeling it possessed, no more, and he groaned. Truth stared at him though natures eyes, the ugliest of his kind, inside and out, an Unworthy without a cloak. She walked the last fifty feet to stare up to a smirk as he opened a cunning, foul tasting mouth, and said, 'Touché.' She smelt the word, reeked in fear and the diamond dagger he stabbed with. She was nature's solution as she side stepped his lunge and breathed out… A flame so pure, he solidified, toasted to ash… She flapped her wings one time. Ash fluttered. The ugly black smell of history disappeared onto the tastebuds of all who saw.

'Tandiette,'her mother's voice close… and by the power invested in her, she changed, as if by magic, back to the daughter she was.

'Who has the key?' she growled her voice not ready to make the transformation her mother deserved.

Devlin stepped forth. The big one. The one she wanted Biscuit to "take out," destroy. He held out the key, dangling, thinking… "Will she take the bait?" In his other hand, an axe, twice her size, blood dried back from a freshly sharpened edge to a firming grip. She blinked and held a breath, to one eye closed. The glare from her, seared clean, his sole ear. It fell softly to sink in the footprints of others as he dropped the axe and bent to one knee, feeling for what was lost, soaking in the dirt of his deeds.

'Now that looks more balanced, don't you think?'

'Yes Mistress,' he growled, eye to eye and placed the key at her feet.

'Well,' she said, 'unlock the cells and free all the prisoners.' Not satisfied, with another breath she let forth her cry 'AAaaiiee', one of three worlds, no matter what form she showed. All creatures great and small bowed their heads, and, the largest amongst the Unworthy lowered his and unlocked the cells.

Seraphina, Radian and Melinda crawled out of the cage. Her mother stood, stretching, before gingerly walking on her bent legs. Tandiette's blue eyes electric, ready, as Devlin released the twins, Parian, Ashland and Claritine. Her mother's voice soft. 'Thank you,' she said as Tandiette remembered, ever so distant, how it felt to have a mother's warm arms wrap her up.

Welled in in a smile she gazed up to her love, tears ready to wash away a big bit of grief. Biscuit's voice running in her head like her own…"And it's knowing we will climb in the memories of our sky, riding wild the rivers of our mind…"

And her mother stroked her head and said. 'I always believed, my beautiful little one.' For a second, she forgot and sank her face into her mother's chest, that was, until the rise of a disgruntled Unworthy yet to know his place. She pulled away, eye's alight as her mother said, 'Go my love, to the songs they will sing, told with the legend of your life, my little young one. Tandiette be thy name, where every critter, dare not complain.'

She transformed and flapped once to stare down as his grumble ceased, lucky not to become a stain of her disdain, a baby's pain too fresh… She grumbled and walked away to the rocky thrown, of sorts, followed by an obedient friend who scampered, ready if needed. Each rock higher she stepped… With feet dangling, she sat atop the Unworthy's seat… Below, a Grand Rous rustled with offerings. Pleading as his fatty face lilted to one side and he reached into a vest and said, 'For you, mistress dragon,' one step back, near tripping over Radian, he laid down a wad of Dearling cash.

Tandiette stared at her gift and said, 'King pig of the Mukbungs with your "fiat" money,' and she breathed out… The fiery remnants, turned to glowing ashen promises, on the cold stone.

Startled he stammered, 'Sorry,' to fumble, and with the twist of three fingers he revealed a gold coin. Her claws retracted and she reached out. Head bowed, eyes down, he stepped up to release the coin into her palm. She looked at the prize and as quick, flicked it in Radians direction. Practised by experience he caught and bit down on the gold sovereign. His smile all she needed to dismiss his majesty with his crown of deceit. Radian teeth all she saw as he crawled to curl under her feet and rest his head on his hands.

From a throne, crowned by the Unworthy, she looked out over her domain and wondered if she was what a stepmother had feared. Then, with Biscuits memories running in her brain, she thought… stay tuned.

The End

Acknowledgements

To my wife, Ann, who patiently listened twice over to every word read, a-loud.

To Mandurah Scribblers for their ongoing support.

To Annie, Lyn and Keith for their editing and opinions.

Other books by Ann and myself:

All the king's horses... paperback and digital

D for destined... Also available in audio... paperback and digital.

To our grand-daughter, Maggie, who wanted to draw her dragon for the book on hearing the first two paragraphs, (see next page).

If you enjoyed reading this book, a review would be much appreciated.

Epilogue

Alone in the mound of a Dearling home
Tortured by the thought of an empty day
Will such things just pass and fade away
Hold me tight with the taste of your ways
Lost to the deeds of fame and taunts
Washed in the void of the great beyond
Who will say... was I to blame
For what am I, the keeper of past bygones
A fiend for all who reign, and you my reason to be
Ribbons to rainbows, dreams to pay, mixed to greed of another day
And if any say I am easy prey, let me be the fiend to interrupt their mis-behave, so they can be scared all over again
Hold me tight by the taste of your thoughts. Lost to the deed of fame and taunt
We burn the same, Biscuit and me, a breed not keen on another's demon seed
Because weak are those that feed on others needs
So beware, I will graze on those who dare

The reckoning

www.ingramcontent.com/pod-product-compliance
Lightning Source LLC
Chambersburg PA
CBHW020406130626
46549CB00006B/2462